Blood in the Snow . . .

As he fumbled with his fly buttons, Mojave Joe glanced at Longarm, who stood holding the gun on him.

"A moment's privacy here, Dog?" Joe grinned. "Judgin' by how them fillies was howlin' last night in the lodge, I didn't take you for one of them *funny* boys."

Longarm had taken only two steps toward his saddlebags before a foot thudded in the snow behind him. There was another thud as something punched his back, low on the left side.

He stumbled forward as the knife was pulled out of his back, the ache sucking the air from his lungs. He heard Mojave Joe chuckle, saw the man's boots behind his own. He set his feet beneath him and wheeled around as the outlaw again lunged toward him. The knife he held in both manacled hands, ripping the slack of Longarm's mackinaw.

The lawman gave a savage grunt as, raising his Colt like a club and swinging it behind him, he smashed the pistol's butt against Joe's right temple. The man grunted as he flew up and sideways and hit the ground on his side, the knife flying out of his hands, bouncing off a rock, and skidding into the snow, which it splashed with dark red blood.

Longarm's blood . . .

DON'T MISS THESE
ALL-ACTION WESTERN SERIES
FROM THE BERKLEY PUBLISHING GROUP

TABOR EVANS

LONGARM

AND THE HAPPINESS KILLERS

JOVE BOOKS, NEW YORK

THE BERKLEY PUBLISHING GROUP
Published by the Penguin Group
Penguin Group (USA) Inc.
375 Hudson Street, New York, New York 10014, USA
Penguin Group (Canada), 90 Eglinton Avenue East, Suite 700, Toronto, Ontario M4P 2Y3, Canada
(a division of Pearson Penguin Canada Inc.)
Penguin Books Ltd., 80 Strand, London WC2R 0RL, England
Penguin Group Ireland, 25 St. Stephen's Green, Dublin 2, Ireland (a division of Penguin Books Ltd.)
Penguin Group (Australia), 250 Camberwell Road, Camberwell, Victoria 3124, Australia
(a division of Pearson Australia Group Pty. Ltd.)
Penguin Books India Pvt. Ltd., 11 Community Centre, Panchsheel Park, New Delhi—110 017, India
Penguin Group (NZ), 67 Apollo Drive, Rosedale, North Shore 0632, New Zealand
(a division of Pearson New Zealand Ltd.)
Penguin Books (South Africa) (Pty.) Ltd., 24 Sturdee Avenue, Rosebank, Johannesburg 2196,
South Africa

Penguin Books Ltd., Registered Offices: 80 Strand, London WC2R 0RL, England

This is a work of fiction. Names, characters, places, and incidents either are the product of the author's imagination or are used fictitiously, and any resemblance to actual persons, living or dead, business establishments, events, or locales is entirely coincidental.

LONGARM AND THE HAPPINESS KILLERS

A Jove Book / published by arrangement with the author

PRINTING HISTORY
Jove edition / August 2008

Copyright © 2008 by The Berkley Publishing Group.
Cover illustration by Miro Sinovcic.

ISBN: 978-0-515-14512-0

JOVE®
Jove Books are published by The Berkley Publishing Group,
a division of Penguin Group (USA) Inc.,
375 Hudson Street, New York, New York 10014.
JOVE is a registered trademark of Penguin Group (USA) Inc.
The "J" design is a trademark belonging to Penguin Group (USA) Inc.

PRINTED IN THE UNITED STATES OF AMERICA

10 9 8 7 6 5 4 3 2 1

Chapter 1

Deputy United States Marshal Custis Long pulled his grulla gelding down off the windswept ridge and, holding his Winchester across his saddle bows, drew to a halt between two snow-laden pines.

Longarm, as he was known to friend and foe, stared down the hill through the pine forest, at an old trading post—roadhouse—a stout, two-story log affair with a broad porch and a corral and stable to the right—spewing sooty wood smoke into the inky, late afternoon shadows of the hollow below.

Beneath the flat brim of his snuff brown Stetson, Longarm's eyes were the same steel blue as the winter snow clouds building beyond the ridge behind him, the eyes of a man whose friend had been cut down in the prime of life by a handful of shiftless drifters who, because they'd had no money for hooch and whores, had decided to rob a stage.

The stage had been driven by Longarm's friend, Buster Davis, out of Alamosa. The drifters had grabbed the strongbox and killed Buster for the simple reason that, as they were about to ride off with the strongbox lashed to a mule, Buster had grumbled that someday they should try working for a living, like decent folk.

One of the robbers—none of the stage passengers had been sure which one—had, without batting an eye, shot Buster in the chest and left him bleeding to death in the driver's box as they whooped and hollered and galloped off across the southern Colorado hogbacks.

Longarm lifted the collar of his buckskin mackinaw, hunkering low against the chill breeze kicking up now at the end of the day, sifting snow from the pine boughs, and drew his gloved index finger taut against his Winchester's trigger.

He studied the two clumps of saddled horses tied to the hitch rack fronting the trading post. There were two sets—one of five horses, and one of four. There were five riders in the party Longarm had been tracking since picking up the killers' trail in Myers Gulch in the foothills of the Sangre de Cristos.

Thinking of Buster's young widow, Marley, and their innocent two-year-old daughter, Willow—the frontier was a cold, lonely place for a young mother alone—Longarm set his jaw and continued staring coldly out from beneath his hat as he heeled the grulla on down the hill, keeping his finger on the Winchester's trigger and weaving amongst the pines.

He bottomed out in the hollow and approached the trading post slowly, the grulla's hooves crunching the hock-high snow, its breath jetting in the darkening air around its head. One of the horses at the hitch rack turned toward the approaching stranger, stomped a rear hoof, and whinnied. Above the cabin's roof, the chimney smoke thickened as someone inside built up the fire against the falling mercury.

Longarm pulled up in front of the hitch rack to the right of the door. He kept his eyes on the windows flanking the porch as he looped the grulla's reins over the peeled-log rack, then, slowly levering a shell into the Winchester's breech and off-cocking the hammer, settled the barrel on his shoulder and mounted the porch steps.

Longarm didn't think the five killers knew he'd been tracking them—they'd given no indication of knowing since he'd picked up their trail two days ago—so he tripped the timbered door's steel-and-leather latch and walked in casually, closing the door behind him and stomping snow from his boots.

The heat from the roaring fireplace was so heavy that it nearly pushed him back against the door, and the smoke was so thick that it nearly sucked the breath from his lungs. Immediately, the frost on Longarm's eyebrows and long-horn mustache melted and beaded as he looked around the room, blinking as his eyes adjusted to the smoky shadows. The screech of a fiddle sounded from the second story, above his head.

The room stretched before him, long and narrow, with a big fieldstone hearth on the right and a long, timbered bar beyond it, against the right wall. There were ten or so tables to the left of the bar and another between the fireplace and the front wall, to Longarm's right.

That table was occupied by four men in drover's garb—flannel shirts, vests, hats, and woolly chaps, blanket coats draped over their chair backs. The smell of cattle wafted on the smoky air around them. They'd all glanced at Longarm, barely looking up from smoking and holding cards, sizing him up with only vague interest. One nodded a cordial greeting, then knocked ashes from his long, Mexican cigar before turning to the others at his table to place a bet.

A table farther back in the shadows, to the left of the bar, was occupied by four more men. One of the men had a girl on his knee. Longarm noticed, as he strolled toward the table on his way to the bar, that all four sets of male eyes were glued to him, squinting under shabby hat brims or through curls of cigarette smoke. These four, too, were playing cards, but their game had come to a dead stop now as Longarm, keeping in the periphery of his vision the men who fit the descriptions of the four killers, sauntered past their table.

In the cracked mirror behind the bar, he watched them scrutinizing him, their faces slack, eyes hard and suspicious. A chubby, redheaded girl in a low-cut, spruce green wrapper sat on the knee of a short, stocky gent in a bowler hat with a grisly, knotted lump of skin where his left ear should have been. The girl's dress was so thin that Longarm could see her pointy, pear-shaped breasts beneath it.

A Spencer rifle leaned against the far side of the table, and a silver-plated Remington .44 lay on the table itself, near a whiskey bottle and the right hand of a long-haired blond with a black eye patch and a tattoo on the nubs of both his leathery cheeks. The two men sitting with their backs to Longarm, turning their heads to watch him, both wore double-holster rigs on their hips, and the bone handle of a knife protruded from a boot well.

These were four of the five men he was tracking, all right. But where was the fifth?

As the fiddle continued to screech above his head, Longarm set his Winchester atop the bar, keeping the four killers in the corner of his left eye and in the mirror behind the bar. He'd have a drink and warm up, get some feeling back in his fingers, before he took them down.

The bartender faced him across the four timbers comprising the bar—a beefy gent with a broad, dark, brown-eyed face, black mustache hanging like miniature horse tails down both corners of his mouth. He wore a smoke-stained, deerskin tunic over his husky torso. A beaded necklace hung low on his chest, the end bulging out with his formidable paunch.

"What will it be, meester?" the man said in a Russian accent. "Beer, wheeskie, wadka?"

"Got any Maryland rye?"

The man stared at him as though he hadn't said anything.

"Wheeskie," Longarm said.

As the big man turned to grab a shot glass off a pyramid atop the back bar, a girl groaned above Longarm's head. "You gonna play that fiddle your whole hour, or you gonna fuck?"

As the fiddle in the ceiling screeched shrilly, then stopped, the big man turned from the back bar with a glass in one hand, a bottle in the other. Bedsprings squawked and the girl chuckled as the barman carefully filled Longarm's shot glass, then set the bottle on the bar and hooked a thumb toward a chalkboard hanging on the wall beside the mirror, upon which was scrawled "Whiskey Ten Sents, Beer Five Sents, Girls One Doller/Hour."

Longarm tossed a silver dollar on the bar, then leaned forward, furtively unbuttoning his coat with one hand while raising the whiskey to his lips with the other. "I might be a while."

"You come far?" the big man grunted, leaning forward and narrowing his brown, slanted eyes. "Long way, uh?"

"Alamosa," Longarm said.

The four drovers lifted a low, conversational hum as they continued playing their poker game, oblivious to the newcomer. But Longarm knew that the four men behind

5

him, with the redhead, had heard him clearly, because they were listening raptly. In the back-bar mirror he could see them peering at him through the wafting tobacco smoke and exchanging edgy glances.

Longarm threw back the shot and gestured for the barman to pour another. Above the heavy ceiling beams, a bed was beginning to get a good workout, the springs sawing and the girl sighing while the man grunted and muttered something too softly for Longarm to hear.

That seemed to ease the tension amongst the killers behind Longarm. Like the drovers, they snickered at the sounds of the lovemaking and, chuckling and muttering and calling bluffs and bets, they resumed their poker game, albeit with a watchful eye on the tall newcomer in the heavy mackinaw standing with his rifle across the bar top.

The redheaded whore sitting on the stocky gent's knee leaned back to inspect his cards and whisper into his ear, stretching her thickly painted lips with a grin. Longarm wished she'd hightail it. He didn't want her to take any lead, and he had a feeling lead would start flying soon. She caught him glancing at her in the mirror, and returned his look with a coquettish bat of her long, false lashes and with a broad, tomato red smile.

Longarm sipped his second drink and waited for the whore to leave. He considered killing some time by stabling his horse—with or without prisoners, he'd be spending the night here—but the killers might split up while he was in the barn, and he liked them just like they were, clumped together and seated.

But without the whore who kept glancing in the mirror at Longarm, running her brash gaze up and down his tall, broad-shouldered frame and fluffing her hair.

Longarm finished his second drink, and as he set the shot glass on the bar with a frustrated sigh, there was the shuffling snap of cards being laid down with a flourish, and one of the killers said, "Read 'em and weep, Giff! This pot's mine, amigo!"

"Jesus H. Christ!" the whore exclaimed, staring down at the pile of coins and certificates in the middle of the table. "Where'd you fellas get all that money?"

A hush fell over the table. The two men facing the bar jerked their heads toward Longarm, and one of the two with their backs to the bar froze in the middle of sweeping the money toward his chest. The man beside him stared across the table at the other two, his back taut.

Longarm didn't move. He kept his chin down, eyes on the mirror. The whore was frowning as she shifted her gaze among the men before her.

"Look," she said, her eyes suddenly skeptical, "I don't care—"

"Where'd we get all this money?" said the long-haired blond man with the eye patch, staring at Longarm's back, lips stretching a snaky grin. He repeated, louder, "Where'd we get all this money?"

The whore didn't say anything. Neither did the other men. The four gamblers at the other table fell silent, as well. The bed upstairs was squawking and the girl was moaning melodramatically while the man fucking her was shrieking, "Ahh . . . Jeezus . . . *ahhhh!*"

"Well, I'll just tell you, Red," the blond killer said. "We got this money here off a stagecoach west of Alamosa, headed for Durango. Sure as shit, we took down the stage and the kid drivin' it. Shot him through the brisket and left him floppin' around the driver's boot like a landed fish, yellin' for help and"—he grabbed his chest with both hands and thrashed around in his chair—" *'Jesus God, they shot me!'* "

Longarm's jaws tightened as, inching his open coat back behind the Colt Lightning .44 holstered in the cross-draw position on his left hip, he began turning slowly around.

Chapter 2

As Longarm turned to face the four killers and the red-headed whore, he hooked his coat back behind the holster that housed his .44. The movement also revealed the silver deputy U.S. marshal badge pinned to his brown leather vest, just to the left of his string tie and below the half dozen three-for-a-nickel cheroots bulging his shirt pocket.

The killers were all turned to face him and, as one, all sets of eyes slid to the badge, and their face muscles tightened, eyes narrowing. The whore's face blanched. The blond man with the black eye patch grinned cunningly.

"Say, now, I thought I smelled the dead-bear reek of federal law!"

The others stared tensely up at Longarm, a couple inching their right hands toward the edge of the table.

Holding the men's gazes, Longarm said mildly to the redhead, "Run along, miss."

The girl began to rise, but the stocky gent, grinning across the table at Longarm and puffing a cigar wedged in the corner of his mouth, snaked his left arm around the whore's shoulders, holding her down. "She stays."

The girl's eyes suddenly filled with horror.

While Longarm wanted nothing more than to turn all four of these men toe-down, like they'd done to Buster Davis, he prided himself on following the law. At least on *trying* to follow the law. That meant he had to give them a chance to throw down their irons and give themselves up.

He sighed. "You boys are under arrest for stage robbery and murder. Keep your hands above the table."

They all smiled. The blond rannie chuckled, inching his right hand slowly toward the silver-plated Remington on the table before him.

"Lawdog," the stocky gent laughed around the cigar in his mouth, "you're outnumbered."

"First one of you reaches, dies bloody," Longarm warned.

In spite of the whore's presence, he felt a grin stretch across his lips. The grins on his opponents' faces suddenly stiffened, and doubt played across a couple sets of eyes like cloud shadows on summer lakes. The stocky gent, glaring at him from beside the terrified redhead's right shoulder, bunched his lips suddenly and dropped his hand beneath the table, his own shoulder falling as he reached toward his hip.

The whore screamed, "No!"

Longarm's right hand whipped across his belly, grabbed iron, and rose quickly.

Pow!

The entire room jumped as the blast echoed off the saloon's stout log walls. The stocky gent hadn't quite raised a brass-chased Colt Navy above the table before Longarm's .44 drilled a neat round hole in the man's pink forehead, just above and left of the bridge of his wedge-like nose.

The whore screamed as the man's head jerked back, pale blue eyes crossing, and threw herself sideways from the dying man's lap.

The shot and the whore's scream hadn't ceased resounding before Longarm, instinctively tracking, shot the man who'd been sitting with his back to him, on the left, as the man bolted up and wheeled with a cocked Smith & Wesson in his fist. As the man flew back over his chair, blood jetting from his neck, the blond rannie bellowed like a poleaxed bull and bounded straight up, throwing his side of the table up in front of him and extending his silver-plated Remy over the top.

At the same time, Longarm saw the other man who'd been sitting with his back facing the bar grab the rifle. He quickly levered a shell into the breech, snapped the butt to his hip, and swung the barrel toward Longarm. The lawman dropped to a knee and triggered the .44 into the third bone button on the man's red and white checked shirt.

The man screamed and fired the rifle into the floor as the long-haired rannie triggered the Remy over the top of the table.

The slug burned across Longarm's left jaw. Longarm pivoted left. The man fired another round across the top of Longarm's right shoulder. As the blond killer moved forward, holding the table in front of him, Longarm fired his double-action .44's last three rounds into the tabletop.

The outlaw threw his head back on his shoulders and dropped the table to reveal three blood-geysering bullet holes forming a perfect triangle over his chest. As he stumbled back, grunting, his eyes rolling back in his head, a revolver barked to Longarm's right, and the slug sliced past Longarm's nose to hammer the front door down at the other end of the room.

11

Longarm jerked around to see a rangy, shaggy-headed, lantern-jawed hombre standing halfway down the stairs, barefoot, wearing only buckskin trousers and a red underwear shirt, suspenders hanging free down his long legs. He extended a long-barreled revolver over the railing and squeezed off another wild shot.

Longarm holstered his empty Colt, reached back, and grabbed his Winchester off the bar. As the tall, rangy man on the stairs lined up another shot, swaying a little as though drunk, Longarm bolted forward. He dove over a table as the rangy man's shot plunked into the puncheons behind him, and Longarm hit the floor and rolled.

Rising up off his right shoulder, he angled the Winchester toward the stairs and fired. The rangy gent flinched as Longarm's slug tore into the unpainted board wall behind him. He returned two more shots as two more of Longarm's slugs plunked into the wall behind the stairs on either side of him.

The man cursed loudly, flinching and cowering, then turned and began running back up the stairs as Longarm jacked and fired three more shots, two slugs plunking the railing while another hit the top railing post as the man turned to flee down the hallway.

As Longarm pushed himself to his feet, gritting his teeth against the burn along his left jaw, feeling blood dribble down his cheek, a girl's shrill scream sounded upstairs.

Longarm cursed, jacked a fresh bullet into the Winchester's breech, and ran to the stairs. He took the steps two at a time, paused at the top to edge a look around the corner, then turned around the angle and moved slowly along the hall.

There were three doors on each side of the corridor lit by a window at the end and by several smoky candles guttering in wall sconces. Longarm moved ahead slowly, holding his Winchester straight up and down and pricking his ears, listening for movement above his own creaking footsteps.

His bulky shadows moved along the walls, angling back and forth behind him. Beyond, the sack-curtained window was nearly dark.

At the end of the hall, on the left side, a door opened suddenly. A girl groaned as she was thrust into the hall in front of the window. She was topless, wearing only a thin pair of panties, her full, pear-shaped breasts screened by her blond hair. The rangy, lantern-jawed hombre moved out behind her, holding a cocked, long-barreled Colt Army to her right jaw. Hunkered low, keeping as much behind her as possible, he smiled grimly at Longarm. He had thick, pewter-colored hair hanging low over one brow, wide-set, ice blue eyes, and a thick, sandy mustache.

"Put the gun down or I'll blow her purty head off!"

"Go ahead."

Both the hard case and the girl widened their eyes with exasperation. The girl was breathing heavily, smooth cheeks flushed with terror, pink nipples peeking through her long, thick locks.

"You fired off six shots downstairs," Longarm said. He narrowed his eyes as he stared down the Winchester's barrel. "But I'm betting you didn't reload."

The man's eyes changed for a half second as he mentally counted his shots.

Longarm squeezed the Winchester's trigger. The man and the girl screamed as the slug ripped into the board wall over the man's right shoulder, powder smoke wafting.

"All right!" the hard case shouted, dropping his arm from the girl's shoulder, tossing the cocked revolver into

13

the hall, and hunkering down against the window, cowering and cursing.

Sobbing, the girl crawled over against the wall to Longarm's right and buried her head in her knees.

Longarm lowered the Winchester to stare down at the man glaring up at him, pewter hair in his eyes. "I didn't shoot that damn driver. That was Heath that done that. You can't hang that one on me."

"Shut up and turn around, wrists behind your back."

As the hard case, growling and cursing, followed Longarm's orders, the lawman glanced at the sobbing blonde. "I'll have this privy snipe out of your hair in a minute, miss, and you can go back to your room. I'll send up a drink to calm your nerves."

A husky female voice, slightly accented, rose behind him. Footsteps sounded, making the floor creak. "It's all right. I will take her to my room."

Longarm, crouching to slap his cuffs around the hard case's wrists, looked over his right shoulder and froze. Was he hallucinating? A black-haired beauty in a long bear coat, open to reveal a white corset, camisole, and pantaloons, padded toward him in light brown, beaded moccasins. Almond-colored breasts pushed up out of the camisole, and long, thick, black hair bounced across her shoulders as the bear coat buffeted about her slender legs.

Longarm clicked the right cuff closed on the hard case's wrist as the woman, in her early twenties and owning an Old World, regal air, crouched down over the girl. She took the girl's hands in her own and gently pulled her to her feet.

"It is all right now. The shooting is finished." She glanced at Longarm, stygian eyes glistening in the candlelight and the fading light from the window. She arched a brow. "Is it not?"

14

"I reckon I'm done," Longarm said, jerking the hard case up.

The outlaw's eyes were riveted, as were Longarm's, on the black-haired woman who was gently shoving the blonde's hair back from her face, hugging the girl gently and cooing to her.

"Where the hell'd *she* come from," the hard case asked no one in particular. "If I'd have known she was around, I wouldn't have wasted my time with the blonde!"

"I am not for sale," the woman said haughtily as, with one hand around the girl's waist, she ushered her toward the door standing open near the stairs, on the left side of the hall.

She stopped and glanced over her shoulder at Longarm, shaking her hair down her back and giving the tall lawman the cool up-and-down before returning her eyes to his face. "That graze on your cheek needs tending. Knock on the door to Room Two later, and I will tend it."

With that, she turned and led the blonde into the room and closed the door behind her.

"Shit." The outlaw laughed. "Wish I woulda taken a burn."

"Shut up and move," Longarm said, prodding the man's back with the Winchester's barrel.

When the outlaw had taken two steps, he stopped and looked down at his revolver on the floor against the wall. "You sure I fired off six rounds down there?"

Keeping the Winchester aimed at the hard case, Longarm crouched to pick up the revolver. Holding the gun in one hand and straightening, he depressed the revolver's hammer and flicked open the loading gate. He turned the cylinder, tipped the barrel up, and shook the gun up and down.

An unspent cartridge clinked to the floor and rolled around the hard case's bare left foot.

"Damn." Longarm chuckled, shaking his head as he flicked the loading gate closed, then wedged the revolver behind his cartridge belt. "I thought for sure you'd triggered six shots down there."

Chapter 3

Longarm had taken three steps down the stairs when the hard case turned around suddenly, head lowered, and bulled back toward him. Longarm had kept four steps between him and the man, so he had plenty of time to lift the Winchester's barrel and ram the butt straight forward. The brass plate and the man's head met with a solid smack.

The man gave a sudden chuff, straightening, eyes rolling back in his head. Hands cuffed behind him, he fell straight back onto the stairs with a thunderous boom. He rolled— *thump, thump, thump*—to the stairs' bottom and piled up against the wall, unmoving.

A picture of a naked girl on a white horse was jolted off its nail to fall facedown on the hard case's slowly rising and falling chest.

Longarm stared down at the man, sighed, then glanced over the rail into the saloon's main hall—smoky and shadowy and with several overturned tables and chairs and the four dead men sprawled in blood pools on the puncheons. The blood and viscera added a coppery smell to the aroma of burning pine, cigarette smoke, wet leather, and wool.

Three of the four drovers stood back by the front door, staring up at Longarm warily. The fourth drover knelt beside the blond-haired outlaw, one arm resting on a knee as he shuttled his gaze between the unconscious hard case at the bottom of the stairs, and Longarm. No sign of the redheaded whore.

The burly Russian barman stood in front of the bar, hands on his hips and glaring up at Longarm, black brows stitched with an exasperated frown.

"Who's gonna pay for this mess?"

Longarm looked at the drover kneeling by the blond man. "Any life left in any of them?"

He shook his head and spat a wad of chew into the sandbox over which the blond outlaw's arm was propped. "They're deader'n dirt."

"Good."

"Who are you?" the Russian wanted to know. "Wyatt Earp?" It sounded like a serious question.

Longarm sighed. "Just a forty-a-month federal out of Denver. Uncle Sam'll send you a check for the damage." He winced when he thought of the tongue-lashing he was going to get when his boss, Chief Marshal Billy Vail, saw the expense voucher. Another broken-up saloon. "I'll be haulin' that son of a bitch back with me in the morning. Wouldn't have a storeroom with a lock on it, would you?"

The Russian glanced at the unconscious hardcase, giving one of his drooping mustaches a thoughtful tug. "There's a cellar in the barn. You can nail the door down." He shrugged as he stooped to pick up a chair. "He'll freeze, and you no worry about him."

Longarm cursed and sleeved blood from his burning jaw as he moved down the stairs. He kicked the unconscious outlaw onto his belly, then grabbing his cuffed wrists, back-and-bellied the man across the barroom floor, kicking chairs and tables out of the way. He pulled him up to a ceiling joist not far from the fire and recuffed his hands around the joist, so that he lay curled up at the bottom of the beam, head resting on the cold floor, drooling.

"There's more than one way to skin a cat," Longarm grunted.

As he went over and began scooping up the money that had fallen off the table, he glanced at the drovers still standing around like shy boys at a barn dance, shuttling their gazes between him and the dead men. "If you boys dispose of the stiffs for me, you can keep their guns and horses. The money on 'em belongs to the stage company in Alamosa."

And to a young *widow* in Alamosa, Longarm thought, though he doubted the stage company would offer any financial compensation for the young mother's loss. Longarm himself would do what he could to help Marley Davis, but she'd have a tough road ahead without Buster.

As the drovers scurried forward, eager to pick the dead men's bones, Longarm resisted the urge to drill another hole through the long-haired rannie's unshaven face. Doubtless he'd been the one who'd killed Buster. He'd had an air of impetuous savagery about him.

He found most of the loot in a saddlebag still hanging over one of the chairs the men had occupied before Longarm had turned them toe-down. Inside the saddlebag was also a small bundle of Wanted dodgers—one for each of the dead outlaws and one for the man snoozing at the base of the joist, whose name, according to the paper adorned with his sketched likeness, was "Mojave" Joe Willoughby.

While the drovers dragged the bodies outside, Longarm stuffed the money from the floor into the saddlebags, then draping the bags over his shoulder, went out to stable his horse and one of the horses from the outlaws' group of five. He'd use the handsome buckskin to haul Mojave Joe back to Denver—on federal charges, as the strongbox he and the other outlaws had robbed had also been loaded with U.S. mail.

As if killing Buster hadn't been enough to hang him.

When he'd tended the horses, Longarm shouldered his own saddlebags as well as those of the outlaws, grabbed his rifle, left the stable, and, wincing against the chill, closed the doors behind him. He lifted his coat collar and started tramping back to the trading post–roadhouse silhouetted against the night's cloudy sky, his breath fogging before him in the chill air, the snow crunching beneath his low-heeled cavalry boots.

Spying movement in a second-story window, he stopped suddenly, automatically raising his Winchester. He lowered the barrel again slowly. It was a woman's figure silhouetted there in the second-story window. She was turned sideways, and he got the full effect of her ample bosom thrust before her—the mysterious, black-haired, full-breasted gal with the Russian accent. She held the curtains back with one hand and bent her head slightly to peer down at him. Lifting her head, she let the curtains close over the window and turned away, disappearing into the flickering, umber lamplight and shifting shadows behind her.

Longarm stared at the window, feeling a lusty pull. He hadn't had a woman since he'd frolicked with Cynthia Larimer, the niece of Denver's founder father, General Larimer himself, in Denver the night before he'd headed out for Alamosa. That had been three weeks ago. He was feeling the itch, but he needed food and sleep more than he needed his ashes hauled. It was a three-day ride back to Alamosa in good weather, and the lowering skies bespoke snow.

Besides, he had a prisoner to guard.

He continued toward the front of the roadhouse, where the four drovers were mounted up, leading the outlaws' four mounts, the outlaws themselves draped over their saddles, hatless and coatless, their hair blowing around in the breeze.

One of the drovers turned toward Longarm and said above a sudden blast of cold wind, "If it's all the same to you, we'll dump these fellas in a draw just over that ridge yonder."

"Wolves and bobcats gotta eat, too," Longarm said, reaching for the door latch.

"We sure appreciate the horses," said the shortest of the four, a paunchy, middle-aged gent with a red and white knit scarf tying his hat on his head. "We come from a small outfit, and extra horseflesh is always appreciated."

He pinched his hat brim, then heeled his swaybacked paint back in the direction from which Longarm had come, jerking a white-socked black along behind him. The blond-haired rannie's arms and legs dangled down both stirrups. The others gigged their horses after the first man, and the men, horses, and dead outlaws soon faded into the thickening evening shadows, heading toward the star-capped, southeastern ridge.

Longarm went in and checked on Mojave Joe, who was still unconscious and in the same position as before. The burly Russian was down on all fours at the back of the room, scrubbing blood with a brush and a wooden bucket filled with soapy water. He gave Longarm an owlish glance as the lawman grabbed his bottle and shot glass off the bar and sagged into a chair.

"I'd help but I'm plum fagged," he sighed, splashing whiskey into his glass. "Is that stew I smell?"

"Got a whole pan of it," the Russian grunted as he scrubbed. He stopped and glanced at the blood on the floor before him. "I was expecting a full house tonight."

"You bring me a plate, I'll pay you for two."

The man straightened his back, wincing. He dropped his brush in the soap bucket and pushed heavily to his feet, grumbling, "I suppose all that shooting makes a man hungry, uh?" Shaking his head and chuckling dryly, he ambled around the bar and disappeared through a curtained doorway behind it.

Longarm threw back the whiskey shot, refilled the glass, and fired a three-for-a-nickel cheroot. Then he sat back in his chair, sipping the whiskey and savoring the stogie. The fire popped in the hearth, and the wind whistled around under the eaves, making the roadhouse's stout timbers creak. Mojave Joe snored softly.

Longarm glanced at the ceiling. The redhead was probably hiding under her bed upstairs. The blonde had gone into the room of the black-haired gal. He remembered the black-haired gal's full figure spilling out of her corset and curving the lines of that bear coat, and couldn't help considering the fact that he was out here in the middle of nowhere, on a cold November night, with three prime lasses and one unconscious prisoner.

He scowled as he sucked cigar smoke deep into his lungs. That was the whiskey talking. No matter how many women were hereabout, and no matter how cold the night, he needed a meal and a good night's sleep . . . alone.

But after he finished the antelope stew and thick wedge of crusty bread, he dropped the spoon in the bowl and

22

found himself turning to the Russian, who was hammering a chair back together atop the bar.

"Seen a black-haired gal upstairs. Your daughter?"

He manufactured an offhand air, throwing back half a whiskey shot and enjoying the glow the whiskey and food spread like warm tar throughout his tired body. But he kept his eye on the Russian, who stopped pounding to peer back at him across the overturned chair, arching his brows devilishly.

"Niece. Her pa-pa and me and her—Anastasia—built this place up from scratch, back when there were still trappers about. She was only six when we came up here from Albuquerque." He winked. "Growed up nice, eh?" He bunched his lips suddenly, scowling like a fighter preparing to deliver a knockout blow. "She is not whore. She is—how you say?—*madame* of the whores. Keeps the books and makes the freight orders. Very smart. Not whore. Very pure, Anastasia. Waiting for the right man to marry."

"All right, all right. I was just curious," Longarm said, chuckling and throwing back the other half of his whiskey. He wasn't sure how pure any girl could be, however, with tits like those he'd seen brazenly escaping out of her corset. "I'd like a room. Mojave Joe'll keep till morning down here."

"Take Six," the Russian said between hammer blows. "No lock, no key." He looked over at Longarm from beneath his shaggy brows. "Only Anastasia's room has a key."

"As it should," Longarm said, gaining his feet and shouldering his saddlebags, muttering, "A girl looks like that . . ."

With two sets of saddlebags on his left shoulder, Longarm picked up his rifle and headed for the stairs, half-feeling his way through the thickening shadows, boots crunching the sawdust the Russian had sprinkled over the bloodstains. "Best keep your distance from ole Mojave Joe," he grunted, puffing his cigar stub. "If you get any more travelers this evenin', you might wanna pass the warning on to them, too."

The man snorted dryly as Longarm headed up the stairs, wincing under the weight of the saddlebags. "You and him might be the last of my business for the whole blame winter!"

As Longarm neared the top of the stairs, he glanced at the door on the opposite side of the hall—the one the black-haired woman and the blonde had disappeared into. Anastasia. The name made his loins itch. As he turned down the hall, he became aware of the bullet burn. The blood had dried. He could feel the thick, congealed patch of it in a parallel line across his jaw.

Keep moving, he told himself, ignoring the ancient, slow burn in his loins.

He was nearly past the door and still puffing the cigar when the door latch clicked. He stopped, turned. Anastasia peered at him through the crack between the door and the frame. Longarm gave a nod, rolled the cigar to the other corner of his mouth, and continued moving.

"Hold on!" the girl whispered in her Russian accent—not as thick as her uncle's, but distinctive in this neck of the woods.

Longarm stopped, turned to her once more. She'd opened the door two feet, and the guttering candlelight reflected in her eyes, which were the molasses brown of a rich stout beer. She wore the bear robe, but no longer the corset. Her full breasts were clearly defined by her tight, white camisole, the nipples pushing out from behind the soft cotton.

The almond skin above the bridge of her nose wrinkled as she whispered, "I told you I would take care of that wound."

"It's no wound," Longarm said, lifting his eyes with effort from her breasts and mentally pushing himself on down the hall. "Just a scratch. I can tend it."

He took one more step down the hall and stopped again when she said softly, huskily, "Not the way I can."

He sighed, turned to her once more, his heart falling while his longhandles became a little more confining across his crotch. She smiled at him, dark eyes flashing, leaning a shoulder against the half-open door. She let the coat hang wide, breasts thrusting against the camisole—large, full, primitive, and undeniably alluring. Behind her, a softly lit room with a big four-poster and a ticking woodstove beckoned.

Longarm squinted an eye and cocked his head. "Your uncle said you were pure."

"He is my uncle. Are you going to come"—she arched a brow and drew the door a little wider—"or stand out there and let my uncle spoil our doctoring?"

"I gotta room . . ."

"Play your cards right, Marshal, and you may not need it."

Longarm turned full around, and, smiling seductively, she stepped aside and drew the door wide. He moved over the threshold and into the winking candlelight and the enticing mixture of smells that included burning pine smoke, incense, and a rich tea that reminded him vaguely of the smell of Mexican tobacco.

The room was small but well-furnished with an ornately carved dresser, washstand, and armoire. It was cluttered with furs and hats and women's clothing and eroding stacks of magazines, newspapers, books, and dime novels, several of

25

which lay open here and there about the mess. On the log walls hung photographs of Russian peasants and primitive paintings and bright tapestries of bucolic country scenes.

Above the washstand hung what appeared, to Longarm's unschooled eye, to be a woodcut of a well-hung black stallion mounting a young woman wearing a frilly peasant's smock and bent over a stone well coping, from behind. He would have studied the picture longer but his eye was drawn to something even more enthralling stretched out atop the big, canopied four-poster.

It was the blonde whom Mojave Joe had used as a human shield. She looked much better now, lounging as she was, head propped on her hand, entirely naked except for a gauzy white wrapper draped about her shoulders and quilts drawn up to her bare knees.

She lay sideways atop the rumpled bed, facing Longarm, a smoky smile on her smooth, porcelain-pale, heart-shaped face with bee-stung lips and blond hair curling about her cheeks. Her pale breasts were exposed between the flaps of her wrapper, and she seemed completely uninterested in covering them.

"Come in," Anastasia said in her faint Russian accent, stepping up beside Longarm and gesturing toward the blonde and the bed. "Won't you join us?"

Chapter 4

Longarm felt a little self-conscious, standing there in his mackinaw and hat and holding two sets of saddlebags and a Winchester, with a pretty, naked blonde smiling up at him from what appeared to be a well-used bed.

What had he wandered into? Was he expected to join the party?

He'd tangled with two women at once a couple of times in the past, and he'd liked it just fine. In fact, he'd liked it real well.

He wasn't sure what to say, so he just rolled the cigar to the other side of his mouth and said, "Hello. Feelin' better now, are you?"

"Much," said the blonde, her cheeks dimpling as she lifted her head slightly and shifted her knees.

Anastasia reached for the top pair of saddlebags on his left shoulder. "Let me help you with those."

"That's all right," Longarm said. "I didn't realize . . . uh . . . that you were predisposed. I'll just be headin' on over to—"

She moved up in front of him and, standing on her bare tiptoes and snugging her breasts against his chest, pressed

27

two fingers against his lips. "The more the merrier. Right Scandinavia?"

"That's what I have always said," said the blonde, squirming around as though she needed to use the privy. Longarm noticed that she, too, spoke with an accent.

"Now, let me help you with those," Anastasia said more forcefully this time, peeling the top set of saddlebags from his shoulders and grunting a little as she set the bulging bags over a chair.

When the outlaws' saddlebags were secure, she took the second set—Longarm's own—and draped them over the chair back. That done, she began helping him out of his heavy buckskin mackinaw. Longarm puffed the cigar, vaguely looking around for a place to throw it while feeling naked himself with the naked blonde, Scandinavia, lying there, grinning up at him like a lioness who'd just been tossed a fresh roast.

His face warmed and his heart skitter-stepped like a high-bred stallion in a Texas thunderstorm.

When Anastasia had hung his coat on an antler stand by the door, she led him by the arm to the bed, turned him around, and gently pushed him down until he was seated on the edge of the mattress, in front of the blonde's bent knees.

"There," the Russian said in her husky voice. "Why don't you take your shirt off while I get some water to clean that graze."

While she moved to the washstand, the blonde bounded up onto her knees, making the bed bounce and shake, and hunkered down beside him, shoving her face right up to his. She placed one hand on his chin, the other on the back of his neck, and turned his head this way and that, inspecting the cut.

"Doesn't look *sooo* bad," she said, her small, round breasts jostling in the corner of his right eye. "You're lucky it didn't catch you an inch deeper, though, or it would have taken off your jaw!" She dropped her hands to her bare thighs. "Did you kill the one with me? Mojave Joe?"

"He's downstairs, sound asleep." Longarm said, resting back on his arms and drawing another puff of cigar smoke into his lungs. "I'll be hauling him off first thing in the morning."

"Look what he did to my arm." Scandinavia held out her right arm, the smooth, delicate skin bruised around her forearm and biceps, for Longarm's inspection. "He couldn't play the fiddle for shit, either."

"I heard."

She scooted around to his left side, then leaned down in front of him and began unbuttoning his shirt, her bare breasts sliding against his arm and shoulder. "We need to get you out of that shirt," she said, her breath smelling like fruity liquor and tea. "Didn't you hear Anastasia?"

"Reckon I got distracted."

Longarm shuttled his gaze between the girl's hands opening the buttons on his shirt and Anastasia, who sat on the bed beside him, drawing her legs up Indian style and setting a tin washbasin on her láp. She dipped a sponge into the water, squeezed it out, and dabbed at Longarm's cut.

She pulled her hand away, arching her brows. "That hurt?"

"Nope." Longarm raised his arms as Scandinavia pulled his shirt off. "Uh-uh."

Anastasia smiled, her lustrous dark eyes slanting, and continued dabbing at the crusted blood as Scandinavia began stripping away the lawman's red, wash-worn underwear top, which clung like a second skin to the twin slabs of his muscular, hair-tufted chest.

"You girls do some mighty good doctoring," Longarm grunted. "I don't have a pain in my whole body."

As the girl began pulling at his underwear legs, he leaned over Anastasia and dropped his cigar in a tin cup on the table to the left of the bed. When he straightened again, Scandinavia said sexily, "Scoot up, and we'll get you out of these silly old things."

Longarm dropped his legs to the floor, pushed up on his butt. Scandinavia peeled the right leg of his underwear bottoms down to his right knee, then the left leg down to the other knee. His dong, now as stiff as an ax handle, bobbed free of the wash-worn woolens and slapped back against his belly with an audible smack.

"My," Scandinavia rasped. She knelt between his spread legs, massaging her breasts with his underwear and staring wide-eyed at his crotch. "Look at that."

Anastasia glanced down at Longarm's throbbing, fully engorged cock angling back over his belly, and arched a black brow. "Judging by the way you fill your trousers, mister—"

"Might as well call me Custis."

"You could have some Cossack blood, Custis." Anastasia lifted the basin of red water from her lap and set it on the floor. Then she slid up close to Longarm, letting the bear robe fall from her shoulders. Smiling at him beguilingly, she crossed her arms and lifted the cotton camisole up from her belly.

She paused as her jutting, pink nipples appeared, teasing him, then continued lifting the camisole up to her chin, exposing the full, heavy, pear-shaped breasts. She lifted

30

the garment up over her head and, as her rich black hair tumbled down across her slender shoulders, she flung the wrapper atop the cluttered dresser on the other side of the room.

Longarm stared at the heavy orbs, his cock so hard that it ached. Her nipples pebbled under his gaze. As Scandinavia leaned forward, placing her hands on his legs, Longarm leaned sideways and kissed Anastasia's left nipple, tonguing it, nibbling it gently until she sagged back on her arms and groaned.

As Longarm placed his right hand on the small of the Russian's back, holding her while he sucked each nipple in turn, Scandinavia snugged her breasts up against his cock, gently massaging him with her cleavage. Anastasia groaned like a female bobcat in full season, arching her back and rolling her head from side to side.

Longarm suddenly felt Scandinavia's full lips close over the head of his member. The hot, wet sensation fired volleys of pleasure bolts in all directions from his loins.

He lifted his head from Anastasia's breasts as the other girl's mouth slowly slid down his aching cock toward his balls.

Anastasia straightened her back slightly and pulled him against her breasts as Scandinavia slid her mouth up and down on his shaft, making wet, sucking sounds and groaning as though someone were pinching her bottom.

"Such sweet pain, is it not?" Anastasia cooed down at Longarm. "Scandinavia knows her work."

Longarm groaned and sighed as he kneaded the Russian's large right breast but lifted his head sharply as his cock hit the bottom of the blonde's throat and, feeling her muscles expand and contract around his bulging head, exploded.

Longarm jerked with the most exquisite convulsion he'd experienced in a long, long time. *"Uhnnn!"*

He gripped the Russian's breast with one hand and held the blonde's head down on his cock with the other. She gagged and choked and, finally, when the last of his seed had finished spurting down her throat, she lifted her head and, eyes squeezed shut, her smooth cheeks mottled crimson, sucked a deep breath between her full, damp lips.

"Jesus, Joseph, and Mary!"

Panting and choking, she pulled away from him and stared in awe at his still-hard member, the base of which she continued clutching in her right hand.

"This one comes like an ox, Anastasia!"

Longarm flopped straight back onto the bed, his bare chest rising and falling.

Anastasia's voice was a pouty, husky purr as she kicked her legs out behind her and dropped to her elbows. "I will judge for myself."

She lowered her head and planted a wet kiss on Longarm's belly. Tired as he was, the touch of the beautiful Russian's lips, the caress of her silky hair on his skin, caused a renewed rumbling in his loins.

He set his hands on her shoulders, pulled her up, then smoothed her rich, black hair back from her face and closed his mouth over hers. Kissing her, he ran his big hands up and down her back.

She dropped a hand to his shaft then lifted her head, smiling, eyes shining in the shunting shadows and smoky candlelight. "You *are* Cossack!"

Longarm rolled her onto her back.

Kneeling on the floor with her elbows propped on the side of the bed, Scandinavia said, "Give it to the horny bitch, Custis!"

Anastasia laughed with excitement as Longarm, with one hand under her back, and with a single thrust of his right arm, slid her up and turned her lengthwise, her head on one of the bed's three feather pillows. As he spread her legs apart with his own, Scandinavia clamored onto the sheets and twisted quilts, her blond hair flying about her still-flushed features, and stretched out beside them.

The girl reached under Longarm, closed her fingers around his jutting shaft, and squealing delightedly, guided it through the Russian's dark-furred portal.

"Ahh-ohhh!" Anastasia exclaimed, lifting her head from the bed as though she'd been stabbed in the belly. Scandinavia chuckled and leaned down to nuzzle the Russian's breasts as Anastasia lay her head back on the pillow, wrapped one arm around the blonde's neck, and dug the fingers of her other hand into Longarm's biceps while wrapping her legs around his back.

"Fuck me, Custis!"

Scandinavia kissed and fondled Anastasia's big breasts then lifted her head to entangle her tongue with Longarm's before hunkering down to watch the mechanics of Longarm's and the Russian's coupling, groaning and grunting as though she were the one getting the shaft.

The lawman had the otherworldy sensation of fucking two women at once. It was one he'd remember on his deathbed, he thought as, after a good fifteen minutes of sweaty toil, his passion rising to a tooth-grinding crescendo, he rose up on his toes to drive as deep as he could.

In the corner of his eye he saw Scandinavia reach behind her, dropping her right hand nonchalantly down over the side of the bed.

"It ain't there," Longarm grunted as he continued hammering between Anastasia's spread knees, which he'd driven up and back nearly to her ears, as she ground her heels into his hips and panted.

Scandinavia froze, staring at him. Anastasia continued panting and sighing as she turned her head toward her cohort.

"The pigsticker . . . you were fixin' to stick in my back . . . is on the nightstand," Longarm told the blonde between hip thrusts.

Hammering away at Anastasia, who continued groaning and moaning despite the sudden anxiety etched on her wide-eyed face, Longarm nodded at the ebony-handled stiletto he'd set beside the Tiffany lamp and the cup in which he'd dropped his cigar stub. He'd seen the handle protruding from beneath the mattress and had sleeved it while the girls had first scuttled up around him, doting on him with improbable zeal, then set it on the night table when he'd dropped the cigar in the cup.

"If you go for it"—Longarm did not alter his organ-grinding rhythm as he lifted a corner of Anastasia's pillow, to reveal his gold-plated, double-barreled derringer—"I'm gonna have to give you a pill you can't digest." He grunted and winced, his blood boiling in his veins, sweat dribbling down his cheeks and into his mustache. "Now, s'pose you go sit in the corner like a good girl, and let me finish what I started. When I've taken my pleasure, I'll take my saddlebags and *go*!"

This last he nearly bellowed as he thrust his hips sharply forward, sinking his shaft deep into the Russian's hot, spasming core. His loins erupted with violent abandon. He groaned and squeezed his eyes shut as he continued thrusting and coming.

Anastasia turned her head from side to side, hair flying, yowling and exclaiming in Russian as she ran her fingers through his hair and ground her nails across his shoulder blades. Her legs were snaked across his back in a bone-crushing death grip.

When Longarm had finished the job and Anastasia let her legs drop down to the bed, she stared up at him, eyes suddenly bright with fury. Her arm snapped up and, in a blur of motion, she slapped him hard with her open palm then brought the same hand back across his other cheek. His member still inside her, Longarm slapped her with the back of his right hand. It wasn't a love tap, and the smack resounded like a pistol shot.

Instantly, the right corner of her lower lip began to swell around the small, vertical cut.

Staring up at him, her eyes flashed black fire. Her cheeks flushed, and her breasts rose and fell sharply.

"Beast!" Scandinavia grumbled from the chair in the corner, about ten feet from the bed. She sat with a wrapper thrown about her shoulders, one knee raised, arms crossed on her naked breasts.

Longarm pulled out of the Russian and rose onto his knees, chuffing dryly. "You two ladies invite a man into your room to fuck him, kill him, and steal him blind—and *I'm* the beast?"

Anastasia sat up against the head of the bed, crossed her arms beneath her heavy, sloping breasts, and dropped her chin like a chastised schoolgirl. "How did you know?"

"You were just a tad too eager to get me in here, and since I was carrying the outlaws' saddlebags, I had a feeling it wasn't only to practice your mattress dance."

Longarm leaned down to remove his derringer from under the pillow. Palming the peashooter, he climbed off the bed, picked up the basin of bloody water, and emptied it into a porcelain thunder mug.

Then, as the two women watched him, both pouting and

35

staring at him with mute, savage fury, he filled the basin with fresh water and gave himself a whore's bath, and dressed.

He had a feeling the women had probably lightened the load and perforated the hide of many a flush, horny traveler. While attempting to rob and kill a federal lawman was indeed a federal offense, he didn't want to mess with hauling their cunning asses to jail. He had his hands full with Mojave Joe.

Besides, it was damn hard for a man like Longarm—who did so appreciate a good ash-hauling, no matter how potentially deadly—to fuck and cuff.

He picked up his rifle, stuffed a fresh cigar in his mouth, and scratched a lucifer to life on Anastasia's dresser. He lit the cigar and, puffing smoke, shouldered the saddlebags and opened the door.

He glanced at the women, who were frozen as before, scowling at him like whipped children.

"It's a sad day when I have to tell such a pretty, talented pair not to fuck and rob anymore—a sad day indeed—but you two behave yourselves from now on, hear? The local sheriff will be calling on you, just to make sure."

With that he dipped his chin, headed out, and closed the door behind him. As he started down the hall to room 6, he heard someone—probably Scandinavia—spit toward the door with an angry grunt.

"That ain't ladylike," Longarm muttered.

Chapter 5

Longarm slept relatively well for a man who'd nearly been screwed to death.

It helped to have his Colt revolver propped on the door latch, and his off-cocked Winchester lying across the chair beside his bed in room 6. Anyone, male or female, trying to enter under cover of darkness would have heard first the slam of the .44 hitting the floor and then the roar of the Winchester an eye-blink before a lead pill shattered their breastbone.

The lawman was done fucking around. He wanted to get the sole surviving member of the gang who'd gunned down young Buster Davis to the judge, jury, and executioner, and he wanted to do what he could for Buster's widow, Marley, and daughter, Willow.

He woke to gray dawn light seeping through the room's single, frost-rimed window and to someone angrily shouting downstairs. Longarm lifted his head to listen, but the only words he could make out through the old trading post's stout timbers were "goddamnit," "lawdog," and "piss."

He recognized the voice of Mojave Joe, and cursed as he lifted his head from his pillow, yawned, and rubbed his eyes. He hadn't undressed but had slept atop the bed in his mackinaw—he hadn't laid a fire in the sheet-iron stove crouched in the corner, either—so he needed only to stomp into his boots, don his hat, and shoulder his gear to make himself trail ready.

Longarm stepped slowly into the dim hall, which was rife with the smell of candle wax and Anastasia's incense. Glad to find no one positioned for an ambush, and Anastasia's door closed, the room behind it silent, he headed on down the hall and began descending the stairs, which were still littered with the wood shards his Winchester had cleaved from the walls and railing.

"Goddamnit, you weasel-faced lawdog," Mojave Joe was yelling from the front of the dim main hall, "wake your ass up and get down here! I gotta take a *piss*!"

As Longarm thumped down the stairs under the weight of his gear, he growled, "Shut up, you murderin' bastard, or I'll give you another hole to pee through."

"There you are, you son of a bitch!" The outlaw sat against the floor joist, his legs curled under him, craning his neck to peer across the room toward the stairs. A fire popped and snapped in the fieldstone hearth before him. "It ain't right, you crackin' my skull, then leavin' me tied to this goddamn post all night. The fire went out, and I damn near froze to death, and I've had to take a piss for the past *five hours*!"

As Longarm gained the bottom of the stairs and started across the room, he saw the big Russian standing behind the bar, forking food off a plate, a stone mug steaming beside him. It was too dark in the room for Longarm to see the man's face clearly, but as the Russian plucked food from between his teeth with one hand, he shook his head and growled, "I've been about to lay an ax handle across his head since he woke me with that caterwaulin' an hour ago!"

"You should have sicced that pure niece of yours on him," Longarm growled as he slumped sideways to let the saddlebags slide off his shoulder and onto a table. "That'd have taken care of it."

The Russian only hiked a shoulder and continued eating.

Longarm fished his manacle key from his coat pocket, then poked the Winchester's barrel against the back of Mojave Joe's head as he crouched behind him.

"Ouch!" Joe exclaimed.

"Shut up," Longarm warned as he turned the key in the lock until both manacles sprang free of the man's wrists. "Now, get up and, for the love of God and all that's holy, please give me a reason not to have to cart your mangy carcass all the way back to Denver."

Mojave Joe told Longarm to do something physically impossible to himself as the lawman cuffed his hands in front of him then prodded him toward the door.

"It's colder'n shit out there," Joe complained. "Let me grab my coat."

"You'll piss faster without it."

Again, Mojave Joe told Longarm to do something physically impossible to himself.

Longarm ordered the Russian to fill a couple of plates for him and his prisoner, then opened the front door and motioned the cursing outlaw outside and around back to the privy hunched in the pines under a two-inch layer of new-fallen snow. While Joe took care of business inside, muttering and sighing and stamping his feet on the floorboards, Longarm stood just outside the door, watching snow flurries continue to fall from a low, leaden sky against which the pines stood like shaggy black sentinels.

A chill breeze swirled the snow and lifted gooseflesh on Longarm's back. The air smelled like cold steel. A storm was probably brewing amongst the tall peaks to the north and east, as storms often did this time of year in the high country. Longarm wanted to get down out of the Sangre de Cristos before he got caught up here for the winter.

At Alamosa, he'd deliver the money to the stage company and check in on Marley and Willow before hopping the train with Mojave Joe for Denver.

He figured he had a good day's ride out of the mountains, then another day across the flat country to Alamosa.

"Come on, Joe," Longarm growled, ramming his Winchester's butt against the door. "Get the hell out of there before you fill the hole!"

Joe extended his hand through the half-moon cut near the top of the door, middle-finger raised. "Fill *your* hole with this, lawdog!"

Longarm jerked open the door, ripping out the locking nail, grabbed the outlaw by his shirt front, and pulled him into the yard, where he tripped over his own boots and fell to a knee with an angry, *"Hey!"*

Longarm tossed the manacles, and Mojave Joe caught them three inches in front of his face. "Put 'em on and quit pissin' around or I'll don my executioner's hat."

Joe chuffed and shook his head as he closed the right manacle around his wrist. "You just got a pure bad attitude, Dog—you know that?"

"Men who kill my friends bring it out in me," Longarm said as he prodded the man back along the side of the road-house.

"Heath killed that driver," Joe said as he moved up onto the front porch. "You gotta watch what ya say to Heath; he's got a short fuse, Heath does."

"Did."

"Well, I reckon that's right, now, ain't it? I hope you're proud of yourself."

"Couldn't be prouder." Longarm opened the door and pushed the outlaw inside, where the burly Russian was setting two plates on a table near the popping fire. "I'd be just as proud to kill you, too, so you best be choirboy polite on the trail to Alamosa. Now, sit down and eat so we can get a move on."

Mojave Joe stopped and turned to Longarm, raising his manacled wrists and arching his brows.

"Best get used to eatin' with the shackles on," Longarm said, tossing his hat on the table and straddling a chair backward. "They ain't comin' off again till you're dancin' beneath a gallows."

When he and his prisoner had finished breakfast, Longarm shackled Mojave Joe to the same post to which he'd shackled him overnight and went out to the barn to saddle the two horses. He brought the rigged mounts back to the lodge then unlocked Mojave Joe's hands and gave him his red and black striped blanket coat, which the outlaw donned before climbing onto the back of his brown and white pinto.

Longarm recuffed the man's hands and tied them to his saddle horn, then tied his ankles together beneath the horse's belly. Then, holding the reins of the pinto, he swung up onto the grulla.

"Christ, what am I supposed to do if you get shot by Injuns or somethin'?" the prisoner groused. "I won't have no way to defend myself or steer my own damn horse!"

"Should have thought of that before you killed Buster Davis."

"You rock-headed son of a bitch!" Mojave Joe shouted, rising up in his stirrups, hands tied snug to the horn. "How many times I gotta tell you—"

"I know, I know," Longarm said, heeling the grulla forward, "*you* didn't kill him. *Heath* did."

"That's a bonded fact!" the outlaw said as Longarm jerked the pinto along behind the grulla.

"You threw in with him," Longarm said, hardening his jaws as the grulla headed back the way they'd come, over their nearly snowed-over tracks from yesterday. "That makes you just as guilty as if you'd pulled the trigger yourself."

The outlaw snarled above the rustling breeze, "Rock-headed bastard. Just you wait, you . . ." He let his voice trail off as Longarm put the horses into a jog-trot across the meadow in which the lodge sat, then started up the ridge through the pines.

The snow continued falling most of the morning as Longarm led the outlaw's pinto up one low ridge and down the other, following an old prospector's trail southwest in the general direction of Alamosa. The sky was low, and, judging by the cold seeping through his boots and gloves and feeling like sandpaper against his cheeks, the temperature was hovering only five or ten degrees above zero.

On the ridges, the cold wind bent the pines nearly double and threatened to blow the riders out of their saddles. The horses balked and skitter-stepped until they dropped into another valley, where the snow was deepening but the wind was mostly heard—whooshing about the ridges—but not seen.

"I gotta stop and take a piss, Dog," Mojave Joe called about two hours after they'd started. They were following a wide, black, cold-looking creek that ran along the base of a forested ridge. "Come on, damn ya. Let me stop and shake the dew from my lily!"

"Hold it," Longarm said, watching the clouds drop lower and lower, so that half the ridge was cloaked in filmy wool. A hawk shrieked. Except for occasional deer and rabbit tracks, that was about all the wildlife they'd seen or heard from.

"I *been* holdin' it, damnit!" Mojave Joe called. "Come on, now. Be reasonable, will you? I'm real sorry about your friend. If I'd had it my way, he'd still be alive. I didn't know I was throwin' in with no killer. Now, if you don't let me pee, after goin' all night without peein', I'm liable to piss my pants and freeze my dick off! It just ain't right to do that to a fellow human being!"

"You got a lot of nerve, Joe, callin' yourself human."

Longarm drew back on the grulla's reins and glanced over his shoulder at the outlaw slumped atop the pinto. Mojave Joe's big, flat-featured face was red from the cold, and his thick dragoon-style mustache was frost-rimed. So was the thick wing of pewter hair dropping low over his left eye. His forehead had welted up in the form of Longarm's rifle butt. His funnel-brimmed hat, coated with snow, resembled furry white felt.

Longarm cursed under his breath and swung down from his saddle. He led the grulla off the trail, barely discernible now beneath the fresh powder, and tied both sets of reins around a young cottonwood. Tramping back to the pinto, he plucked his folding barlow knife out of his coat pocket and opened it.

"Where the hell'd you get the 'Mojave' handle, Joe?" he asked as, reaching up, he sawed through the cord lashing the man's manacled wrists to his saddle horn.

"Army," Joe said. "Cut me down sixteen Mojaves with a Gatlin' gun back in '69."

"Women and children, most like," Longarm grumbled as he crouched to cut the twine tethering the outlaw's boots together.

"Not all," Joe said reasonably, clamping his cuffed hands to the horn as he swung his right leg over the horse's butt. "But some . . ."

As, standing, the man turned to face Longarm, his red cheeks and snowy mustache shaping a grin, Longarm aimed his .44 at the outlaw's belly. "Get to it. Drain the dragon, then get back into the leather. If we're out here much longer, you're going to freeze more than your dick."

Mojave Joe manufactured a pathetic expression as he extended his wrists. "Couldn't I please get you to remove the cuffs, Mr. Lawdog?" He canted his head and crumpled his eyes. "Pretty please? With sugar on top?"

Longarm just stared at him from under his own snowy hat brim and thumbed the Colt's hammer back with a ratcheting click that sounded inordinately loud in the wintry silence.

The outlaw turned the corners of his mouth down, then shuffled sideways and dropped his cuffed hands to his crotch. As he fumbled around with his fly buttons, he glanced at Longarm, who stood holding the gun on him.

"A moment's privacy here, Dog?" He grinned. "Judgin' by how them fillies was howlin' last night in the lodge, I didn't take you for one of them *funny* boys."

Longarm stepped back and, depressing the Colt's hammer, turned toward the dun. He figured he'd give each horse a handful of grain, because they wouldn't be stopping again anytime soon. But he'd taken only two steps toward his saddlebags before a foot thudded in the snow behind him.

There was another thud as something punched his back low on the left side.

Not a punch, he realized as a searing pain bit him sharply.

A stab.

He stumbled forward as the knife was pulled out of his back, the ache sucking the air from his lungs. He heard Mojave Joe chuckle, saw the man's boots behind his own. He set his feet beneath him and wheeled as the outlaw again lunged toward him, the knife he held in both manacled hands ripping the slack of Longarm's mackinaw.

The lawman gave a savage grunt as, wheeling, raising his Colt like a club, and swinging it from behind him, he smashed the pistol's butt against Joe's right temple. The man grunted as he flew up and sideways.

He grunted again as he hit the ground on his side, the knife flying out of his hands, bouncing off a rock, and skidding into the snow, which it splashed with dark red blood.

Longarm's blood.

Chapter 6

Longarm saw the knife in the snow but he felt as though it was still in his side, probing, twisting, burrowing deeper.

His lower left back was on fire, the pain so sharp that he dropped to one knee, holding his fist against the hole in his coat and scowling down at Mojave Joe, who lay unconscious before him. The man was on his side, head on his curled arm, hat off, blood dribbling across the forehead from the gash in his right temple.

Longarm was sorry to see that the man's chest rose and fell slowly. The bastard had nine lives.

The lawman shuttled his gaze to the knife, the bone handle buried in the snow, the bloody blade glistening faintly in the wan light.

Where had he gotten that? Somewhere in the lodge, no doubt. Or maybe he'd had it hidden in his saddle. Wherever it had come from, he'd obviously hidden it up his sleeve for the right opportunity.

Longarm cursed himself for a damn tinhorn. He knew better than to turn his back on a prisoner. He was lucky he hadn't gotten his fool throat cut. Pressing his coat against his back with his gloved fist, he felt the warm blood seeping out of the wound and soaking his shirt and coat.

He pushed off his knee, ambled up to his horse, and began unbuttoning his coat. Awkwardly—the fire in his side flamed higher when he twisted his back—he shrugged out of the coat and threw it over his saddle. Leaning forward against the coyote dun, which snorted and twitched its ears as it sensed the man's anxiety and smelled the blood, he removed his right glove and then reached around behind to probe the bloody wound.

Finding the hole, he stuck a finger partway in, sucking a sharp breath through his teeth as the pain sharpened. He couldn't tell for sure, but it didn't feel that deep—maybe only a couple of inches. The brunt of the pain seemed to be coming from a rib, which had probably deflected the blade from his kidney.

He'd been hurt worse falling off his horse.

He rummaged around in his saddlebags, produced a bottle of Maryland rye and a roll of blue gingham he used for bandages, and tore off a four-foot length, again sucking a sharp breath as pain flared through him. Removing his neckerchief, he wadded it up in his right hand, soaked it with the whiskey, then reached around and pressed an end over the wound.

The searing, tooth-gnashing pain was like a fist to the solar plexus, conjuring a string of curses as, quickly, he drew the long bandage taut around his ribs and tied it, biting his lower lip.

He took a long pull from the bottle and leaned forward against his saddle.

There. That should stop the bleeding until a sawbones could sew him up. He didn't let himself dwell on his slim chances of finding a sawbones before he reached Alamosa, a good day and a half away.

"Joe, I could kick your ass," he growled, turning to glare down at the outlaw, who'd rolled onto his back now, his chest rising and falling more sharply than before, squinting his eyes and showing his teeth at the pain in his head.

Longarm dropped his bottle back into his saddlebag, drew his Colt, and walked over to the half-conscious outlaw. "Get up."

Mojave Joe groaned and turned his head from side to side.

Longarm kicked him in the ribs.

Mojave Joe groaned louder.

Longarm triggered a shot into the snow two inches to the right of the man's nose.

Mojave Joe jerked with a start and lifted his head, shaking it. "Ahhhh . . . ohhh . . . Jesus Christ . . . you damn near killed me, you bastard!"

Longarm triggered another round into the snow near Mojave Joe's head.

The man jerked away from the shot, raising an arm as if to shield himself from another bullet.

"You got exactly ten seconds to get yourself belly-down atop that horse," Longarm barked. "If you're so much as a half-second late, the next one's going through your balls!"

Ten minutes later, Longarm was mounted and jerking the pinto along behind him, over the saddle of which Mojave Joe lay belly-down, manacled hands tied to his ankles. The outlaw complained plenty, but the wind was building, swooshing the snow and creaking the trees, so Longarm was at least spared the brunt of the man's castigating pleas for forgiveness and mercy.

Longarm rode stiff-backed at first, denying the pain. Slowly, however, as the constant jarring and jostling increased his fatigue and agony, he found himself slumping low over the horse's neck, as though his hat were made of lead.

Aggravating the situation, the snow continued to fall, until he could no longer see the trail he'd been following. He gave the coyote dun its head and hoped the horse—a government remount from an outpost near Alamosa—could sniff it out.

The bloody coat chilled him, and several times he realized his teeth were clattering and willed them to stop. The horse clomped forward through the snow, snorting and blowing against the cold, twitching its ears, wanting a warm bed, hay, and water.

Over one foggy peak and down the other he rode, jerking the pinto and the finally silent Mojave Joe along behind him. Pines, spruce, and firs pushed up close to the trail, then fell back. He glimpsed a lake through a naked aspen stand and skirted a couple of creeks. He scared up a golden eagle, which winged—a large, ominous shadow in the grayness—over a rocky ridge and out of sight.

Stopping the horses in a deep crease between forested ridges, he reached behind and fished his Maryland rye from his saddlebag. He popped the cork, began lifting the bottle to his lips, and stopped.

Ahead, to the right of the trail, a notch opened in the forest. Just before the notch, a wooden sign stood, leaning slightly, flanked by a large, cracked boulder and capped with snow.

Holding the bottle in one hand and frowning curiously, Longarm gigged the dun forward, then drew rein again in front of the sign. Burned into the whipsawed board stretched over the top of an inverted pine log were the words ROAD TO HAPPINESS. An arrow pointed up the narrow, dark notch stitched with swirling snow.

Faintly on the wind, Longarm detected the smell of burning pine wafting down the notch.

"I'll be damned," the lawman muttered, lifting the bottle to his lips and taking a long, soothing pull.

Happiness was no doubt a mining camp, named with the wry humor customary of rock breakers throughout the frontier. Mining camps usually boasted a sawbones or two. At the very least, he'd find a warm room in which to tend his wound and wait for the storm to play itself out.

He took one more pull, studied the sign once more, then hammered the cork back into the bottle with the heel of his hand. "I reckon you can't go wrong, takin' the road to Happiness."

He glanced back at the pinto, hanging its head and blinking against the swirling snow. Mojave Joe was lying silent and still across the saddle, spurred boots hanging just below the horse's belly.

"Come on, boy." Longarm gigged the coyote dun past the sign and into the notch, jerking the pinto's reins in his right hand.

The notch was narrow and rocky, sometimes a two-track wagon trail, sometimes merely scabs of snow-dusted granite exposed by eons of spring erosion, when the trail was likely a millrace sluicing snowmelt down to the San Luis Valley. In a couple of places, Longarm had to rein the horses wide around fallen trees.

He crossed a low saddle, the wind nearly blowing him out of his own, and started down the other side. He glanced right of the trail, then back again, his eyes holding on a large, dead pine trunk standing alone on a rocky bench littered with sun-bleached deadfall logs and obscured by windblown snow.

The trunk's bark had long since weathered away. At the spear-shaped top, from which lightning had probably torn the crown, a large crow sat staring toward Longarm. The bird lighted suddenly, flapping its broad wings and cawing raucously above the moaning, whining wind.

It wasn't the tree or the bird that interested Longarm. What had caused him to check down the dun were the two dead men hanging from the trunk's sole, knotted branch stretching out to the left like a single, deformed arm. One man was in his mid-to-late twenties, the other maybe in his forties—lean, short-haired, and unshaven.

The most distinctive thing about them was that they were both naked. Birds had been working on them, turning their eye sockets and private parts to dark, bloody mush, which meant they'd probably been hanging there for at least twenty-four hours, two days at the most. Any longer than that and their faces would be in worse shape and the birds would have started pecking through their belly buttons.

As the wind nudged them this way and that, they resembled two drunks up far too late and dancing to two different fiddles in their heads.

Longarm squinted against the wind. "The road didn't end happy for those two."

Unconsciously touching the butt of his Winchester sticking up from under his right thigh, he gigged the dun forward, trailing off down the bench and into another canyon. He rode thirty yards down from the crest of the next saddle and halted the horses once more, staring down the trail toward the town nestled below amidst high, craggy, black peaks and scattered pines.

At the base of the peaks on both sides of the town, shanties and dugouts of all shapes and sizes were strewn amidst the rocky hills, and here and there sluice boxes snaked off toward creek bottoms. From his distance of sixty yards or so, and through the buffeting curtain of wind-jostled snow, Longarm saw no movement around the shanties or the false-fronted buildings sheathing the main trail, and he would have thought the town was deserted but for the occasional whiff of wood smoke and the intermittent tinkling of a lone piano.

Longarm grunted as another spear of pain stabbed up and down his back from the knife wound. Holding his head down against the snow blowing up under his hat brim, he urged the horses on down the ridge. As the dugouts, shacks, and placer debris began pushing up along the trail, wood smoke issuing from occasional battered stove pipes, the coyote dun gave a celebratory whinny at the prospect of a warm stable and oats.

Alongside the road, another crude, snow-blasted sign announced: WELCOME TO HAPPINESS! in drippy, hand-painted letters.

Longarm kept a tight grip on the reins, holding both mounts to a fast walk as he cleaved the town's business district, the two- and three-story log buildings and false facades and signposts rising around him. He could hear the piano clearly now, mixing with the squawk of wind-jostled shingle chains, thumping window shutters, and the clomps of his and Mojave Joe's horses on the snowy, frozen-rutted street.

Longarm swung his head from left to right, raking the typical mining camp buildings with his eyes, looking for both a jailhouse and a doctor's office. He took note of a livery stable and corral on the street's left side, then turned his head right to see the only two people he'd seen on the street so far—a woman in a wheelchair and a big, beefy man with long black hair and flat Indian features.

They were out on the veranda of a three-story log structure whose facade above the porch roof announced in large, gaudy red letters: Miss Sylvania's House of Ill Repute.

The woman, bundled in a buffalo coat and a black scarf, with silver-streaked black hair piled in two tight buns atop her head, sat her wheelchair near a large wooden bird feeder. The big Indian in a long bear coat stood beside the feeder, holding a tin cup high before his right shoulder. It appeared to be mounded with seed. Chickadees and nuthatches were swarming around the porch, with several lined up on the porch rail, obviously awaiting a meal.

Both the old woman and the big Indian stared toward Longarm as the lawman pulled the dun toward the porch, Mojave Joe's pinto clomping along behind and blowing, the outlaw himself still residing belly-down across the saddle.

As he drew up in front of the porch, Longarm could see the old woman's pinched, wrinkled face, dark eyes behind small, round, steel-framed spectacles. Both she and the big Indian stared at him stony-faced as the wind plucked seeds from the top of the Indian's mounded cup.

"I'm lookin' for the jail," Longarm said as the piano music emanated from the building's dark windows and the half-open front door. "And a sawbones, if you got one."

"You're scarin' my birds," the old woman said, glancing at the black-and-white chickadees and metallic blue nuthatches flitting around the porch, some careening as high as the roof to sweep low once more, chittering raucously beneath the moaning wind. "They're hungry and cold."

"I know how they feel."

The woman blinked, glanced up at the big Indian, who

54

could have been carved from granite, then turned her dark eyes again to the lawman after a quick glance at Mojave Joe. "On down to the end of the street, other side of the general store. Don't recollect if the sawbones is still here."

With that, she gave a distasteful wrinkle of her nose, then setting her jaws, glanced again at the Indian, who raised the cup to the feeder and tipped the seeds into the wooden tray. The birds shrieked as though with applause, several lighting on the opposite side of the feeder from the Indian.

"Obliged," Longarm muttered, reining the dun away from the porch and into the street, the pinto blowing and shaking its head behind him.

The street, which was only about a hundred yards long, dropped slightly and curved. On the left, a sign announcing TOWN CONSTABLE jutted from the low roof to a pole by the hitch rack. Longarm reined up to the small log hovel with two barred front windows. Swinging heavily down from the coyote dun, he moved back to the pinto, cut the cords tying Mojave Joe to the saddle, then grabbed the man's coat and pulled him down.

His boots hit the ground, but his knees buckled and he fell to the snow on his back, groaning loudly and cursing. "Ahh, Jesus Christ, you son of a bitch! You damn near killed me!"

"On your feet!"

Longarm kicked the outlaw's ribs. As the man writhed, the lawman grabbed him by his coat collar and, ignoring the pain in his back, half dragged him up the stoop's single step to the front door.

Longarm rapped his knuckles against the door's unpainted, whipsawed planks. It swung inward with a squawk. Frowning curiously, he pushed the door wide, peering in to the room's musty shadows and noting a small drift of powdery snow on the earthen floor beyond the threshold.

"Anyone here?"

Longarm's voice was swallowed by the darkness within, which the gray light pushing in behind him barely penetrated. Dimly, it revealed three jail cells at the back of the building's single room, beyond two desks, a few chairs, a sheet-iron stove, a gun rack, a cot, and a stack of split cordwood.

A couple of heavy winter coats and hats hung on the rack in the corner to his right, but there was no other sign that anyone had been here for several hours. The place was as cold as a root cellar. He'd ask around later for the constable. At the moment, he just wanted to get Mojave Joe secured behind bars, thaw out, tend his wound, and rest.

He jerked Joe to his feet and prodded him inside with his pistol barrel. The man stumbled drunkenly, hatless, hair mussed about his head, and his ears red as a firebox, into the far left cell, the only one whose door stood open. Longarm closed the door, found a key ring on a wall nail, and turned the unoiled locking bolt with a grinding click.

Inside, Joe sagged belly-down atop the cell's single cot, groaning and cupping his gloved hands to his ears, his entire body quivering like a leaf in the wind. Having ridden hatless and belly-down for the past two hours, the man was probably nearly frozen solid. Longarm couldn't help taking pleasure in the man's pain. He'd start a fire soon, if only for himself.

First he had to tend the horses.

As he'd ridden up to the jailhouse, he'd spied a crude shed and corral on the rise out back—probably the stable for the constable's mounts. He headed outside and led both horses through the gap between the jailhouse and a general store to the tin-roofed stable across a small, dry gulley bridged with heavy planks.

The stable itself wasn't much, and the wind mewed between the unchinked logs, but nonetheless it was a shelter with hay and oats, and the single trough held water under a quarter-inch crust of ice. Longarm chipped through the ice with a pitchfork handle before unsaddling both mounts, giving them a quick rubdown, forking fresh hay from a pile near the back, and dumping a coffee can of oats into their trough.

He was mildly surprised that no horses were stabled here, in spite of two- or three-day-old apples spotting the straw. The constable might have been called out of the camp, or maybe he had a stable at home.

As Longarm moved toward the half-open door, he stopped suddenly. A man's hatted head and bearded face pulled quickly back from the opening. Boots thumped on the frozen ground, running footsteps clomping across the plank bridge and dwindling into the distance.

Longarm pulled his Colt out from under his coat and, frowning, moved to the door.

Chapter 7

Longarm pushed the stable door wide and, extending the cocked Colt out from his waist and squinting against the pelting snow, looked around cautiously.

Scuffed boot prints shone in the snow around the door, overlaying his own and leading back across the gully toward the gap between the jailhouse on the left and the general store on the right, from the roof of which thick, white smoke tore on the wind.

Keeping the revolver out in front of him, Longarm followed the prints to the mouth of the gap, and stopped. The trail swung right, onto the high porch of the general store. Longarm climbed the steps himself. At the top of the snow-covered loading dock, the prints led to the store's front door.

He peered in the big window to the right of the door, shielding the glare from behind him with his left hand, then pulled the door open and stepped inside as the bell above the transom jingled raucously.

The old man, standing before a roaring, black, bullet-shaped stove and the half dozen gents gathered around it and behind the bar to the right, swung toward him. The oldster's blue eyes nearly bulged from their sockets, and he tugged on his beard as if trying to climb it.

He wore a wool watch cap, long duck coat, and high-topped mining boots, all sporting snow, as was his beard.

"You the spy?" Longarm said, aiming his Colt at the old man's middle. Longarm figured the man was in his fifties or sixties and, stoop-shouldered and wattle-necked, he couldn't have weighed much over a hundred pounds.

The oldster just tugged on his beard and made little high-pitched mewing sounds in his throat.

"Ebeneezer's just nosy," said the tall, black-haired gent in armbands behind the bar cluttered with glass display cases and over which hung cured hams, roasts, sausages, and several recently skinned rabbits and chickens. "Stranger rides into a mining camp during a storm—especially one haulin' a man belly-down over a saddle—Ebeneezer tends to get ants in his pants till he satisfies his curiosity. I, on the other"—glancing at Longarm's Colt, the tall, gaunt man hiked a shoulder and bunched his lips—"can't say as I care one way or the other."

The other men lounging around the stove, fur coats hanging off their chair backs and hot drinks in their fists, stared at Longarm warily. None appeared to be armed. They were all younger, or in one case older, versions of Ebeneezer—hairy, scarred, leather-skinned rock breakers no doubt practically from birth.

As scared as he appeared, Ebeneezer couldn't deny his curiosity as he shuttled his pale blue gaze between the Colt's maw and Longarm's face. "A . . . a lawman . . . is ya?"

Longarm depressed the hammer and lifted the barrel. "That's right." He glanced at the man behind the counter, whom he took to be the general store proprietor, and canted his head toward the jailhouse. "Where's the constable?"

Holding Longarm's stare, leaning forward with his fists on the counter, the man's gaunt, hollow cheeks flushed slightly.

"He done hauled ass out of the mountains," said one of the men around the stove, a freckle-faced redhead with a thick, cinnamon beard and long, crooked nose. He wore a red-and-black plaid shirt under an elk-skin vest with a dark blue, polka-dot neckerchief.

The others turned their heads to the redhead with expressions running from fear to surprise to silent reproof.

The redhead dropped his chin guiltily and sipped from his steaming tin cup, saying softly and with an air of half-hearted defiance, "Left about a month ago."

"No one's replaced him?"

When he received only silence and a couple of shrugs in reply, hot liquid sloshing down wrinkled throats, he opened his coat and hooked his thumbs behind his cartridge belt. "Who hanged the two men north of the camp?"

They all just stared at him. The redhead took another preoccupied sip from his drink. Ebeneezer wheeled nervously away from Longarm and, throwing his watch cap onto an empty chair, grabbed a split log from the wood box beside the stove, opened the stove door, and chucked it inside.

The conflagration stabbed out from the door like a dragon's breath. The stove ticked while the wind howled in the flue.

The man behind the bar, still flushing, said grimly, "Whiskey sling, Sheriff . . . ?"

"Marshal," Longarm growled, letting his suspicious scowl rove across the men hunkered by the stove, then up across the timber-planked bar to the tall, gaunt, black-haired gent regarding him stiffly. "Deputy U.S. Marshal

Custis Long." He moved up to the bar. "How 'bout a doctor? Got one of them in town, or did he haul ass out of the mountains, too?"

"As a matter of fact, he did," said the proprietor. "On the heels of the constable, as a matter of fact. The doc *always* leaves about this time of the year, before the real snow flies. We got a Chinaman that does all the bonesettin' an' such, but Mi-Lee's up at Lake Santos, helpin' with a birth. By the looks of this weather, he won't be back for a day or two." He canted his head toward the jail. "Your prisoner ailin', is he?"

Longarm ignored the question. "Give me a bottle of whiskey and a roll of bandages. I'll take one of them rabbits, too, and potatoes, if you have 'em."

As the proprietor turned away to begin filling the order, he glanced over his shoulder at Longarm, smiling stiffly. "Fixin' to stay awhile, are ya?"

"Till the storm blows out." Longarm winced as he turned to put his back to the bar, nudging the wound, which he could feel bleeding again—icy fingers sliding down his lower back under his balbriggans. "I hope I ain't intruding."

It didn't take a clairvoyant to suspect that something was amiss around here. Prospectors were a reclusive, distrustful lot, wary of all strangers, so their prickly reception of a strange lawman wasn't suspicious in and of itself. But it was damn strange for a constable to hightail it out of the mountains before someone else could take his job.

Who were the two dead men? Why had they been hanged?

Longarm doubted he'd learn anything more here, no matter how hard he pushed. Besides, he had his own wound and his prisoner to tend for the moment.

When the general store proprietor had filled his order,

he took the burlap bag and, glancing again at the men sitting in grim silence around the roaring stove, only Ebeneezer casting him a fleeting, furtive glance from beneath a lock of silver brown hair, he headed back outside, the bell clanging raucously behind him.

He stepped out onto the loading dock and cast his gaze about the street, which was darkening slowly now as the afternoon waned. The snow was coming down even harder than before, drifts piling up against stock troughs and hitch racks, half-burying boardwalks in front of the log buildings lining the street.

The street was deserted. Most of the shops appeared closed. All but the three-story whorehouse, that was—Miss Sylvania's House of Ill Repute. It sat about fifty yards away on the other side of the street, barely discernible through the heavy veil of wind-churned snow. The tinny notes of the untuned piano careened through the walls to mix eerily with the sighs and groans of the storm.

Longarm thought he heard a woman's shrill laugh, or maybe it was just an off-struck key. Whatever the sound, Miss Sylvania's place was rollicking in spite of the squall, prospectors having probably gathered there when they saw the storm clouds had rolled in. There were worse places to ride out a storm—a jailhouse, for instance, with a loudmouthed hard case.

Longarm swung the bag over his shoulder, descended the loading dock steps, and headed back to the stable, where he checked on the horses and grabbed his bedroll, rifle, and saddlebags. Tramping back through the gap between the buildings, he pushed through the jailhouse door. Squinting into the room's rear shadows, he saw that Joe was in the same position he had been in when Longarm had left, only now he was snoring into his pillow.

Glad the outlaw was unconscious—Longarm would rather listen to the man's snores than his threats and insults—he set his possibles on one of the room's two cots, against the left wall, then set his rifle behind the desk. He kicked the snow before the door back outside before lighting a lamp against the gathering darkness and grabbing an old newspaper and some feathersticks from the kindling box.

He opened the door of the sheet-iron stove, which sat in the center of the room, arranged the feathersticks over the crumpled paper inside, then jostled the damper knob, surprised to find that when the constable had left for the last time, he'd left the damper open.

The man must have left in an all-fired hurry.

Again thinking about the men swinging from the dead pine north of town, Longarm scratched a lucifer to life on the stove door and touched it to the paper inside. When the paper and feather sticks were flaming well, he added a couple of sticks from the kindling box, and kept adding the sticks until the fire was large enough to support a couple chunks of split pine from the fragrant stack behind the desk.

Those two fellas hadn't hanged themselves. Who had hanged them, and why? If everyone was as tight-lipped as the boys in the general store, Longarm would probably never find out. And he had no cause to investigate, as there was no reason to believe any federal laws had been broken.

His only job was to get himself and Mojave Joe back to Denver.

The stove ticked and popped and the fire inside made a whooshing sound, filling the room with soothing heat. Even in his sleep, Mojave Joe must have felt the cold recede, for he gave several comfortable sighs between his long, guttural snores.

Longarm set coffee to brewing with the charred, bent percolator on the stove's warming rack, using water from his canteen and beans he found on a shelf near the door, which he hammered and ground with his pistol butt.

As the coffee gurgled and chuffed, Longarm shrugged out of his coat, hung it over the desk chair, and removed his shirt, undershirt, and the bandage he'd wrapped around his waist, wincing as the sticky cotton pulled away from the bloody slit in his lower left back, just below his rib cage.

"Goddamnit," he growled beneath Mojave Joe's rising and falling snores and the wind's keening in the chimney pipe. "I oughta wake you up for a pistol-whipping, you black-souled son of a bitch!"

He tossed the bandage into the stove, then cleaned the wound as well as he could with another whiskey-soaked neckerchief from his saddlebags. The burn traveled all the way up his back, through his spine, and into his heart and lungs, and he had to restrain himself from unsheathing his .44 and squeezing off a couple rounds in the direction of Joe's contented snores.

When he'd wrapped a fresh bandage around his waist, he cut the blood-drenched underwear top free from the bottoms, then pulled on a spare undershirt and wool over-shirt from his saddlebags. Leaving the shirttails untucked, he set about locating an iron pot, filling the pot with water, then chopping up the rabbit, potatoes, and onion, dumping it all into the pot, and setting the pot on the stove to boil.

The stew cooked and the room got toasty and fragrant with the food and burning pine aromas. Outside, the storm pelted the log walls with wind-driven snow, and the wind itself keened witchlike under the eaves and up and down the chimney pipe.

Inside his shadowy cell, Mojave Joe snored and chuckled dryly while muttering about some girl named Loretta.

Outside, wolves howled. The mournful cries seemed to be both carried and muffled by the weather.

Longarm sat in the swivel chair behind the desk and, waiting for the stew to cook, had a couple of stiff shots from the whiskey bottle, then poured himself a cup of hot coffee and added a liberal jigger of hooch. He'd been so busy tending the fire and his wound that he hadn't noticed the desktop. A bottle of India ink was spilled on it, the ink itself frozen and hard where it dribbled off to the right of the blotter and down the outside of the desk. A black pen lay beside a peach can containing several pencils and a letter opener, the point of the pen's nib broken off.

No matter how much in a hurry the constable had been before hauling ass out of Happiness, you'd think he would have at least cleaned up his mess first.

His lawman's curiosity piqued, Longarm took another sip of the whiskey-laced coffee and looked around at the desk. Sliding his gaze to the right, he noticed a large, loosely wadded paper lying beside the small, square, wood-plank trash can on the floor to his right. Wincing again as the stab wound pained him, Longarm reached down, plucked the paper off the floor, then leaning back in the chair, slowly opened the paper on his lap. He folded the corners back carefully and frowned.

The sheet was a Wanted dodger on which the slit-eyed likeness of some hard case named Spike "Hangdog" Squires had been inked—a Wanted circular like the hundreds of others sent to law offices across the West each year. When Longarm could find nothing distinctive about this one, he turned the sheet over.

On the back, in heavy black ink and in a childlike hand, was scribbled:

My deerest Madeleine,

*Soon now you and me shall take our leev
of this tarible place. If you can only
hold out for*

The *r* in the "for" at the end of the clipped missive trailed off in a black ink splotch, just above which was a small tear in the paper, as though the writer had been suddenly, unceremoniously interrupted.

Chapter 8

Longarm picked up the pen, ran his thumb over the broken nib, and glanced again at the small, pin-like tear in the back of the Wanted dodger. No doubt the pen had been used to write the missive, though the writer had stopped abruptly.

Longarm ran his gaze along the floor. Several deep scuffs marked the hard-packed dirt, with here and there slashes that appeared to be made by spur rowels. A spool-back chair behind the room's other, smaller desk, positioned against the opposite wall, lay overturned and broken on the floor.

He looked at the two coats on the tree before him—a red and green mackinaw and a thick sheepskin with a cowhide collar, a black knit scarf hanging beneath it. A battered sugarloaf sombrero and a water-stained, gray Stetson hung from the rack's other two forks, as did a pair of soiled woolly chaps missing several tufts of wool.

Cold-weather gear. It had been cold up in this high country for several weeks, so it was doubtful that anyone would head outside without a coat.

In his mind, Longarm saw again the two dead men

hanging from the pine tree, and his blood quickened. He had assumed they were claim jumpers, or prospectors whose own claim had been jumped, or someone caught screwing the wrong prospector's daughter, but Longarm's lawman's mind couldn't help trying to make a connection between them and the apparent fracas that had taken place in the jailhouse.

The edgy silence of the loafers in the general store only aggravated his suspicions.

Maybe he could find the Madeleine of the unfinished letter written on the back of the Wanted dodger, and get some answers.

"Jesus Christ, can't a feller get nothin' to eat around here?"

Mojave Joe's shout echoed around the small, cluttered room and caused Longarm to jerk with a start. He turned to see the man glaring at him through the cell bars, a savage snarl on his unshaven face, yellow teeth showing beneath his thick pewter mustache.

"I got rights, goddamnit!" he yelled. "You gotta feed me or let me go!"

Longarm stood heavily, the wound stretching and aching, and rummaged around the shelves near the door till he found a couple of wooden bowls and two rusty, food-encrusted spoons.

Returning the prisoner's glare, he slopped the rabbit stew into a bowl and moved toward the cell. The look in his steely gaze must have registered every ounce of his bitter contempt for the man. The angry sharpness faded from Joe's eyes. He blinked, swallowed, and uncurling his fingers from the bars on either side of his face, stepped hesitantly back away from the door.

Longarm stared at him for a beat, then thrust the bowl

and the spoon through the feeding slot. "Here. Take it. If I hear another peep out of you tonight, you're gonna be one federal prisoner who had the misfortune of falling victim to an accidental beating with an ax handle."

With that he went back to the stove and filled his own bowl. He sat at the desk and ate and thought about Madeleine and the two dead men and the missing constable, and all he heard from Mojave Joe was the tick of the spoon against the man's bowl and hungry slurping sounds rising from his throat.

Was Madeleine in trouble?

Mojave Joe muttered once about how a sip of whiskey would sure taste good, but when Longarm continued eating and staring at the unfinished note on the desk before him, the outlaw fell silent.

His cot creaked. He sighed. Soon, as Longarm finished his second helping of the stew and poured himself a fresh cup of coffee and whiskey, Mojave Joe began sending up snores once more, barely audible against the stove's roar and the thrashing, ticking wind.

When the lawman had finished his drink, he banked the stove and unrolled his soogan atop the cot against the room's far wall. He was tired from blood loss and the long, cold ride. He'd be glad to get Mojave Joe to the train station in Alamosa, glad to get his visit with the grief-stricken widow of Buster Davis behind him.

And though it was his dead stage-driver friend and Marley and Willow he thought about as the howling wind shepherded him off to sleep, he dreamt about a young woman named Madeleine rowing a boat far out on a morning-misty lake. Wolves surrounded the lake, and Longarm, who didn't seem to have a gun or didn't think of using it, ran along the shore, trying to get the girl to safety while she continued slipping away in the fog, toward the howling wolves on the lake's opposite shore.

He couldn't see her face, but only the long, dark curls of thick hair falling across her slender, naked form as she rowed away from him.

There were other images and fragments of images and bizarre scenes featuring the faceless girl with the exotic French name, but nothing Longarm could remember clearly the next morning when he opened his eyes to the blue gray light penetrating the barred front windows.

Longarm lifted his head from the pillow, blinked. The wind whooshed and creaked the wall timbers. Snow continued to pelt the walls and windows but not with the same vehemence it had last night. The room was cold as an icehouse, and though he was fully clothed under two wool blankets, gooseflesh covered his body and his jaws were shaking, teeth clacking together.

The knife wound throbbed and he could feel cold, jellied blood matting the bandage. Part of his chill was no doubt from the wound, his body fighting infection.

The pain reminded him of his prisoner, and he turned to peer into the cell. Mojave Joe was a dark lump on the cell's single cot, his snores audible between wind gusts.

Longarm dropped his legs to the floor with a groan, rose, stomped into his boots, then opened the stove's damper and set about building a fire. In the pot on the warming rack, there was still a good bit of stew left over from last night— it had congealed to a near-frozen lump under dark yellow rabbit fat.

Mojave Joe heard Longarm moving about and immediately began barking for food. As though remembering Longarm's savage stare of the night before, he softened the barks to unctuous pleas, then, sighing, took a long piss into his thunder mug.

Later, when Longarm had fed his prisoner as well as himself, downing two cups of fresh coffee, only one of which he laced with wound-soothing whiskey, he rebandaged his back, built up the fire, and shrugged into his coat.

Outside, dawn was in full swing, though the clouds sat low and the breeze had a sharp, cheek-burning edge. It was a cold, silent, black-and-white world. Fresh snow lay in scalloped drifts against boardwalks and stock tanks, and Longarm had to kick through the three feet that had piled up like a frozen wave in front of the jailhouse door.

To his left, a young coyote was chasing a jackrabbit around a rock beneath a sprawling spruce.

It looked like the weather was going to keep him here another day. Just as well. He felt compelled to find out who the two dead men were and if the girl named Madeleine was headed in the same direction.

Longarm looked up at the roof of the general store. The building's chimney was spewing smoke into the flurry-threaded air.

He went around behind the jailhouse to the stable, tended the two horses, who were weathering the cold well despite the fact that their water had frozen once more, then tramped back up through the gap. He mounted the general store's loading dock, the top of which had been swept clear of snow, and was glad to see the OPEN sign in the window.

He pushed inside, the bell jangling over his head, and stomped his feet on the hemp rug just over the threshold as he raked his gaze across the room crowded with shelves and display racks of every shape and size.

In the middle of the room, the big, black stove roared just as it had yesterday. This early, however, only two of the five men from yesterday afternoon were hunkered down around it, faces still red from the outside cold, steaming mugs in their hammy fists. The gaunt, black-haired proprietor stood behind the bar, filling a widemouthed pickle jar with cigars from a small box open on the counter before him. An uncorked bottle stood near the box, as did a steaming mug.

"That wouldn't happen to be rye, would it?" Longarm asked as he moved toward the bar, feeling the owly stares of the two men sitting around the stove.

The proprietor had stopped his work to stare in his own pugnacious fashion from beneath a wing of disheveled black hair. "Bourbon."

"Damn." Longarm sighed as he set both his gloved hands at the edge of the bar. "Oh, well. A mug of hot mud should cover the taste. Why don't you give me one of them and splash some of that panther piss into it? It's so cold my blood feels like the northernmost stretch of the Missouri River in January."

The proprietor poured some whiskey into a stone mug, slid it across the bar to Longarm, then dipped his head toward the big, black pot coughing and chugging on the stove's warming rack. "You pullin' out today?"

Longarm glanced out the windows on either side of the door as he moved to the stove. "Looks like the snow's gonna keep comin'. It'll probably really start to drop when the temperature rises. Must be well below zero out there now."

"That mean you're stayin'?" grumbled one of the seated men—a barrel-waisted, double-chinned gent wearing a fur hat and a curly salt-and-pepper beard.

"Wouldn't want me to freeze on the trail, would you?" Longarm grinned woodenly as, using a thick leather swatch, he lifted the pot from the stove and filled his cup. The coffee steam wafting up was tanged with bourbon.

The barrel-waisted gent recrossed his ankles under his chair and lifted his mug to his lips. "Just wonderin'."

Longarm set the pot back on the stove, then walked around and straddled a chair between the fat man and the other seated gent, an oldster with the dark brown eyes and flat cheeks of a half-breed wearing a red and green knit cap with a fuzzy white ball at the peak.

The lawman rested his forearms across the chair back and sipped the potent belly-wash. "Yeah, I'll hang around a day or two more, wait till the storm's done played itself out. The snow'll be deep in those valleys, and I don't want the horses to fight through it in the cold."

He sipped the java once more and said with an offhand air, "That'll give me a chance to look in on an old friend I heard had thrown down here in this happy little village. Madeleine's the name." He glanced at the man on either side of him and then at the proprietor behind the bar. "Anyone know her?"

The proprietor stared at him from under the disheveled wing of hair once more. The other two stiffened almost imperceptibly. They knew he'd gotten her name from the jailhouse.

Longarm looked around at the men, arching his brows as though innocently awaiting an answer.

The proprietor's dark eyes shuttled to each of the men sitting beside Longarm, faintly admonishing, then returned to Longarm himself. "You must be thinkin' of Crystal City. I never heard of no Madeleine around here." He glanced at the other two men again. "You boys?"

The oldster was flushed like a freshly baked brick. "Nope. Never heard o' such a woman."

"Like Walt says," growled the barrel-waisted man, extending his coffee mug toward the bar, "you must be thinkin' of some gal over to Crystal City."

Longarm looked around once more, then shrugged and sipped his coffee. "That must be it."

He sat back in his chair, dug a three-for-a-nickel cheroot from his shirt pocket, and scratched a lucifer to life on his thumbnail. He hiked a low-heeled cavalry boot onto his knee and sat smoking and drinking the bourbon-laced coffee, taking his time, enjoying the obvious discomfort of the men sitting around him.

None of the three said anything. The two near Longarm sat scowling at the stove and sipping from their own mugs, while the proprietor stocked the shelves behind his counter, casting occasional tense glances over his shoulder at Longarm.

Outside, wolf howls rose clearly in the gauzy gray silence. Small, bead-like snowflakes swirled and ticked against the window glass. The roaring fire pushed the cold back against the overstuffed shelves lining the general store's walls.

A couple of horseback riders, wrapped against the cold, their scarves white with frost, moved along the street—probably lone ranchers or prospectors looking for company. Otherwise the town beyond the store's loading dock appeared deserted.

Longarm threw back the last of his coffee, stood with a casual sigh, and set the mug on the countertop. "Obliged for the drink. I'll be back for grub later. You can add the drink to my tab."

Lifting his mackinaw's collar, he nodded to the men

sitting tensely by the fire and strode toward the door. He thought he heard one of them give a relieved chuff as the bell jangled and Longarm stepped onto the loading dock glazed with a quarter inch of freshly fallen snow.

He pulled the door shut and, holding his coat collar closed at the neck, glanced up and down the deserted street. The tracks of the recent riders were already obscured with snow.

On the other side of the street to his right, the big Indian he'd seen yesterday with the wheelchair-bound woman stood on the stoop of Miss Sylvania's House of Ill Repute. He was scooping more seed into the bird feeder, while the chickadees, nuthatches, sparrows, and several other winter stayers stitched the air around him, screeching. One of the horseback riders whom Longarm had seen passing the general store was walking toward the whorehouse from the livery stable, hunched in his mackinaw, woolly chaps flapping against his thighs.

"I need me a warm woman, Little-Boy!" the man yelled, white teeth showing in his brick red face. "Can you fix me up?"

The big Indian turned to the approaching waddie stiffly and said in a deep, gruff voice, "Always have, ain't we?"

As the waddie took the porch steps two at a time and clapped his gloved hands together eagerly, the Indian turned back to the feeder, into which he dumped another scoop of birdseed.

The waddie pushed through the whorehouse's front door and closed it behind him. Longarm watched the Indian toss another scoop of seeds into the feeder. Then, dropping the cup in the barrel against the front wall and sliding a wooden lid over the barrel's top, he ambled heavy-footed to the door and disappeared inside.

Longarm studied the dark-timbered, three-story building hunched darkly against the cold. The birds had descended upon the feeder, cackling and quarreling and flicking seeds in every direction. Smoke rose from two stone chimneys crawling up both sides of the building.

Longarm rubbed his jaw with a gloved hand.

Madeleine had the ring of a whore's name.

He moseyed down the steps of the loading dock and angled across the street toward Miss Sylvania's House of Ill Repute.

Chapter 9

Hoping to find the girl named Madeleine and the identity of the two dead men, Longarm mounted the porch steps of Miss Sylvania's House of Ill Repute, tripped the brass door latch below the carved wolf-head knocker on the heavy timbered door, and stepped across the threshold and into a warm, dim, surprisingly comfortable, ornate world of rich tobacco smoke and the molasses-like aromas of good liquor tinged with feminine perfumes.

As though the well-populated place didn't know what time it was, the din of conversation rose from tables adorned with elegant cloths and at which a dozen or so burly men sat, playing cards, a couple with gowned young women on their laps or hovering at their elbows.

A couple of gents sat at the bar on the room's left, one with his head on his arms, while a bartender with pomaded hair set shot glasses and beer schooners on the tray of the blonde standing on the other side of the mahogany from him.

She'd caught Longarm's eye, and smiled, showing a mouth of fine, white teeth. In spite of the outside temperature, she wore nothing more than black net stockings, a pink corset, a black choker, and black and purple hair ribbons. She slid her shoulders back, and held her large, creamy breasts straight out in front of her while wagging a bent knee and running her eyes up and down Longarm's tall, broad frame.

Longarm pinched his hat brim toward her and started down the three steps from the risen entryway. A man he'd barely noticed sitting in a chair before him and to his left, in front of a peeled-log ceiling joist, turned toward him abruptly, rising, a belligerent scowl on his broad, mustached face.

The young man wore checkered slacks with spats and a checkered vest over a yellow silk shirt, a neckerchief of the same color knotted around his bulldog neck and pierced with a ruby stickpin. Rusty red hair peeked out from under his crisp bowler hat, and a silver hoop ring hung from his right ear.

"Hey, who the hell are you, fella?"

He held a hide-wrapped bung starter in his right hand and slapped the club threateningly against his left palm while scrunching up his tiny, mean, narrow-set eyes. He moved toward Longarm with the air of a bull resisting a loading chute, barking, "I asked you a question!" As he rose to the second step, he rammed the bung starter toward Longarm's chest as though to impale him. "No one gets in here less'n—"

Longarm swept his left hand up sharply, grabbed the bung starter around its middle, and jerked sideways while driving his gloved right fist straight forward from his shoulder. It struck the man's broad, freckled nose with a resolute smack and crack of breaking cartilage.

"Ach!" The man stumbled back off the step and, holding his nose, fell to his butt with a loud thud.

The man lowered his hand from his bloody nose and, sitting on the carpeted floor, legs bent before him, shoved his face toward Longarm, features flushed with fury, jaw hard. He opened his mouth to speak, but he was cut off by a loud, cackling laugh that echoed around the room like duck quacks in a corn crib.

Longarm looked around to see the woman in the wheelchair parked in front of the broad, fieldstone hearth just beyond the bar on the left side of the room. Her head was thrown back on her shoulders, mouth drawn wide. Laughing, she wheeled herself around a couple of tables and a gilt-embroidered couch angled right of the fire, and headed toward the front of the room.

"Cody, you always was more fart than force!" the old woman bellowed at the man Longarm had so unceremoniously seated. "Now, look—you went and got your beak broke!"

She threw her head back and broke out in a fresh chorus of ear-numbing exclamations.

Movement behind her caught Longarm's eye.

The big Indian stood in the open doorway at the far end of the room, just to the left of a broad, carpeted staircase, an armload of split wood in his brawny arms. He was so tall that he had to bend his head forward at nearly a forty-five-degree angle to keep from raking the top of the door frame.

He frowned toward the commotion at the front of the room, dropped the wood around his ankles, then kicked through the logs as he strode forward, gritting his teeth and bunching his fists at his sides.

"Stand down, Little-Boy," the old woman said, stopping the big Indian in his tracks about halfway across the room. She turned to Longarm, smiling, showing a row of false, yellow teeth under her red-painted upper lip. "The marshal here done culled my floor herd, that's all."

The big Indian shuttled his dark gaze between Longarm and the man on the floor, then turned slowly, casting another dark glance over his shoulder and stomping back toward the wood he'd left on the floor.

The room had gone silent, the loungers and cardplayers of both sexes staring toward the door.

The old woman looked down at the man on the floor, who was in the same position as before, glaring up at Longarm as his nose swelled like a wagon hub.

"Get on upstairs, Cody. You ain't fit for workin' the door. Suppose he'd been Crazy Ed or that damn Norwegian, Karl Karlsson." The laughter had disappeared from her round, prunelike face, to which she'd applied too much powder and paint, giving her the look of a three-day-old corpse. "Git upstairs!"

Cody cursed into his cupped palms, then, pushing off the floor with one hand, rose awkwardly. He cast Longarm a hateful parting glare, then turned and slogged off toward the stairs at the back of the room.

"And don't get no blood on my rug, damnit!" the old woman admonished.

Cody dropped his head lower, elbows moving closer to his sides as he cupped his hands more tightly to his face.

The woman turned her gaze to Longarm and once more her dark eyes flashed with humor. "Need a job, Longarm?"

Longarm ignored the question. "We've met?"

"Nah. But word travels fast in a mining camp." She turned the wheels of the creaky chair, and as the card games and conversations resumed, though most eyes continued shuttling curiously toward the big lawman in the buckskin mackinaw, the old woman spun her wheels toward the bar.

"Get on over here and name your poison, mister. I got more grizzly piss and busthead than the Longbranch Saloon in Dodge City. Summers, I cater to flush sonso'bitches of every stripe."

She paused by the bar to throw up her beringed hands, indicating the grizzled men around her smoking, drinking, laughing, and fooling with the whores. "Winters, I'm left with these reprobates who wouldn't know good whiskey from mink spray." She stopped, swung sideways, and canted her head toward the bar. "Go ahead—what's your heart's desire this snowy morn?"

The dapper bartender in a crisp white shirt, armbands, and clean apron regarded him expectantly with liquid, cobalt blue eyes. The only thing unkempt about the gent was a three-inch half-moon scar under his left eye.

Longarm set an elbow on the counter as he stared bemusedly down at the old woman. "Wouldn't have any Maryland rye on one of them shelves, would you?"

"Shit!" the old woman scoffed, pulling her powdered, wrinkled cheeks back in a self-satisfied smile. As the apron turned toward the ornate, mirrored back bar, she said, "Lewis, splash out some o' that beaver drool for me, too, will ya?"

Turning to Longarm, she shielded her mouth with her hand and rasped none too quietly, "That's Lewis. He don't like girls, so don't stand too close or he'll pinch your ass!"

She threw her head back once again, laughing her wild bobcat laugh.

The bartender flushed slightly, smiling, as he glanced across the mahogany at Longarm, then popped the cork on the Maryland rye and expertly filled two shot glasses. Longarm stuffed his gloves in his coat pockets and gave one of the drinks to the woman, growling, "Obliged for the warning."

He picked up his own drink and raised it toward the woman. "Miss Sylvania, I assume?"

She raised her own drink. "Salute!" She threw half the shot back then handed the shot glass to Longarm. "Grab the bottle and mosey on over here. Take a load off, big fella, and tell me what bad luck drove you to this canker on the devil's backside."

As the woman wheeled herself up to a cloth-covered table near the bar, Longarm grabbed the bottle and, holding both shot glasses in the palm of his right hand, tramped over to the table. He set the bottle in the middle, set Sylvania's glass in front of her, set his own shot glass on the table's opposite side, and sank into the leather-padded chair before it.

He glanced around the room behind Sylvania Thayer and wondered if any of the three lovely doves in sight would answer to the name Madeleine. Another was moving slowly down the stairs at the back of the room—a young mulatto in a tan wrapper that delectably complimented her dark-skinned features. Her chocolate hair was coiled in several loose buns atop her head, and large silver rings dangled from her ears.

Madeleine?

"The storm brought me here," Longarm told the woman, raking his gaze back to the table as the mulatto sashayed over to the bar, where the young waddie in woolly chaps stood, facing her and grinning. "I'm on my way to Alamosa with that prisoner you saw sleeping in his saddle yesterday afternoon. He and his gang robbed a stage, killed the driver."

"Will men ever outgrow their evil ways?" Miss Thayer said, shaking her head and lifting her shot glass. Over the rye glistening in the light cast by candles and oil lanterns, she said with a slight upward quirk of her painted mouth corners, "So, you want your ashes hauled, big fella? You came to the right place for it. I keep nearly a full staff of pussy on over the winter. If I let 'em go in the fall, it's too hard to get 'em back in the spring." Her smile broadened. She threw back the rest of her drink and set the glass on the table. "Purtiest, cleanest doves in the southern Rockies. You can't go wrong."

"I could think of worse ways to wait out the storm." Longarm threw back his own drink and leaned forward to refill Miss Thayer's empty glass. He tossed a furtive glance at her as he splashed out the good rye and said with an off-hand air, "Got one named Madeleine, do you?"

Longarm refilled his own glass, then set the bottle in the middle of the table. Lifting his shot glass, he glanced around the bottle at the crowlike old woman scowling back at him, her cheeks a shade more powdery than they were a few seconds ago.

"Madeleine?" she croaked.

"Heard you had one named Madeleine."

"Where'd you hear that?"

In the corner of his eye, he saw the Nancy-boy apron staring at him while drying a glass behind the bar.

"Oh, don't remember," Longarm said, sipping his drink. "Maybe in one of the other camps I rode through on the way up here." He grinned lasciviously. "It's sort of a name you remember—Madeleine. French-sounding."

The old woman studied him, frowning, as he took another casual sip of the pleasantly warming rye. Finally, she said, "Madeleine's busy. Got her one of the shop owners upstairs. Wealthy bastard. I got plenty of girls as good at givin' French lessons as Madeleine."

85

She turned her head to the side, peering back over her shoulder at the blonde serving drinks at one of the card tables. "Casey, get over here."

The blonde set a beer schooner in front of a man in an elk-skin tunic. "Comin', Miss Thayer."

The girl pranced over to stand beside the old woman's wheelchair, placing a hand on the back of the chair and cocking a hip seductively, smiling smokily across the table at Longarm.

"Casey here gives the best blow jobs around. And look at them tits."

The blonde's pale, plump cheeks colored slightly as she lowered her eyes bashfully and nibbled her bottom lip.

"Casey, open your corset, show the man your tits."

The girl—she couldn't have been over seventeen—set the empty tray on the table. Staring seductively at Longarm, she slowly unfastened the whale-bone buttons and peeled the flaps of the corset back toward her arms.

Both floury white breasts, the size of ripe cantaloupes, bounced free, pink nipples angling slightly outward.

"Biggest tits in the place. Couple those with the girl's facility with French, and, well, you'll not find a better way to pass the storm." The old woman glanced up at the girl still holding her corset open for Longarm's inspection. "Casey, have Mona take over for you, and—"

Longarm cleared his throat, cutting her off. "No offense to Casey—them there's the finest set of orbs I've seen in a long, cold while—but I did sorta have my mind set on Madeleine."

"Madeleine, Madeleine!" the old woman barked. "You're a stubborn badge-totin' son of a bitch, ain't ya?"

"When I get somethin' in my head, there's just no gettin' it out!"

The old woman pursed her lips and looked up at the blonde, who'd covered her breasts with the corset and was now scowling indignantly at Longarm, her eyes firing hazel daggers. "Casey, go up and get Madeleine. Tell her to get down here."

The girl snapped her head toward Sylvania Thayer. "But . . ."

"You heard me. Tell her customer I'll make it up to him with a couple of free blow jobs. Now, skedaddle!" She stared fiercely up at the girl frowning down at her. "Get Madeleine!"

Chapter 10

The blond dove hesitated, chuffed, and holding her corset closed, gave Longarm another indignant glare before wheeling away from Sylvania Thayer and stomping toward the rear of the room. She climbed the stairs in a huff and was gone.

"If you don't mind, Mister Partic'lar," snapped Sylvania Thayer, wheeling herself back from the table, "I got work to do. For Madeleine, I charge six dollars an hour. In a moment, you'll see why—and them's even my winter rates! When you're through takin' your pleasure, pay Lew at the bar."

She gave a disgusted chuff then swung around and headed back toward the fire, which she'd been tending when Longarm had first entered the whorehouse.

The big lawman unbuttoned his coat, sagged back in his chair, careful not to put too much pressure on his left side, and sipped the rye, the one grace note in this trek through the southern San Juans. Imagine Maryland rye this far off the beaten path! To afford such hooch, Miss Sylvania must do a rollicking business.

But if all the whores looked like the three he'd seen so far, he could understand why.

Longarm had taken his last sip of the rye and was vaguely wondering if he could add his time with Madeleine to his expense vouchers when movement on the stairs caught his eye. He stretched his gaze across the dim, smoky room, and the breath caught in the back of his throat.

If the creature descending the stairs—a tall, slender girl with rust red hair piled in delicious swirls atop her head— was indeed Madeleine, at six dollars an hour, he was getting a buy.

She moved down the steps, kicking out each high-heeled shoe with graceful aplomb, running one long-fingered, pale hand along the rail to her left. Her brown eyes sparkled as they swept the room, her head holding when they found her client near the front door.

As she bottomed out in the main hall and moved toward Longarm across the flowered carpet, Longarm watched her creamy breasts jiggle up from beneath her wine red corset edged with black lace. Her filmy black wrapper winged out around and behind her as she turned around tables, catching the eyes of several cardplayers, all of whom fell silent, dropping their jaws in primal appreciation.

The redheaded goddess shaped a sultry smile, her gold-flecked brown eyes sparkling in the shunting lantern light as she approached the table and extended her hand. "Are you the marshal?"

Longarm felt like a kid approaching his first time with a real woman. His ears must have been as red as a prairie sunset as he awkwardly gained his feet and took the girl's hand in his. "Call me Longarm. I hope I'm not bein' unduly pesky, but you come highly recommended."

Somehow there seemed not a speck of arrogance in her demeanor when she said, "Of course I do," then clutching his hand in hers, wheeled and began pulling him gently back toward the stairs.

Longarm grabbed the bottle off the table. As he crossed the room half a step behind the elegant girl, feeling as big and clumsy as a rogue grizzly at an English tea, he glanced to his left. Sylvania Thayer had her back to the room and was prodding the fire with an iron poker while the big Indian added more split wood to the pile abutting the hearth.

Longarm had to remind himself of the questions he wanted to ask Madeleine as he followed her up the stairs, admiring the womanly curves enticingly visible through the gauzy black wrapper flying out around and behind her, which he had to be careful not to step on. He was here to talk, not fuck, but he saw no reason why the two had to be mutually exclusive.

"Right this way, Marshal," Madeleine said as they approached the top of the stairs and moved down a narrow hall elegantly papered in red and gold, candles smoking in wall sconces. "I mean," she added quickly, pausing to brush her shoulder against his, "Longarm."

As they continued down the hall, men's and women's laughter emanated from the closed doors around him, as did the squawk of bedsprings and a man's labored sighs while a girl intoned with false passion, "Ohh . . . oh, *God*!" Behind another door, a girl said in a sympathetic voice, "It's all right, Norman, it'll happen next time—I just *know* it will."

The ceiling creaked above Longarm's head, and he heard a high-pitched, angry voice in a language he thought was Chinese. There was the squawk of bedsprings and a man's muffled, guttural laugh.

To Longarm's left, a door opened. A short, wiry gent about sixty years old with a gray beard stumbled into the hall, chuckling and holding his rabbit hat. He turned, and the girl behind him, dressed in only high-heeled shoes and night ribbons, threw her arms around his scrawny, wrinkled neck as she intoned huskily, "Don't make it so long next time, all right, Jedediah? It ain't right for you to go deprivin' a girl of such wit!"

"Right here." Madeleine had stopped at a door on the right side of the hall, about halfway down. She gave Longarm a sultry smile as she pushed it open and stepped inside. She swung gracefully around to one side, sort of half hugging the door.

Longarm followed her in, doffing his hat and glancing around at the small room dimly lit by two small, sashed windows through which gray light emanated and against which snow ticked. A candle burned on a dresser against the far wall. To his right lay a bed with rumpled quilts and sheets. The faint, sweet, cloying smell of opium hung in the air, mixing with the rose-and-sandalwood aroma of perfume.

The girl threw the door closed and reached up to help Longarm out of his coat. She hung both his coat and hat on the coat tree near the door before turning toward him with the alluring smile of the well-bred whore. It didn't look one bit practiced on this girl's beautiful, oval face with dancing brown eyes and a slight mole off the right corner of her fine wide mouth.

She glanced at the bottle in his hand. "Can I pour that into a glass for you?"

"Only if you'll join me, Miss Madeleine."

"Love to."

As she moved to a table near the dresser, she gestured

toward the fainting couch against the wall, opposite the foot of the rumpled bed. Longarm sat down, wincing again at his back but also at his pants drawing taut across his crowded crotch. The girl's delectable wares, the warm, cozy environs, and the contented glow he felt from the rye had conspired to make him hornier than a young bear stumbling fresh from his cave on a sunny spring morning.

The girl filled two shot glasses, then chucked a couple of split logs into the small stove crackling and ticking in a corner. Plucking the drinks off the dresser, she moved over to the couch, gave one of the glasses to Longarm, then planting a hand on his thigh, sank down onto the floor between his knees, curling her long legs beneath her. She glanced at his well-filled crotch and lifted her eyes to his, raising her mouth corners slightly and narrowing her eyes.

"Comfortable?" She sipped her drink and ran the tip of her tongue across her upper lip. "Or would you like me to take it out and suck it?"

The question, complemented by the appearance of her rosy tongue, was like an injection of pure lust into his veins. His cock throbbed against his pants, straining his fly buttons.

He threw down half his rye. His voice was slightly pinched as he wriggled around on the couch and said, "I got a confession to make."

The girl sipped her own drink. Staring up at him with those lustrous brown eyes lit by the pearl gray light emanating from the window flanking Longarm, she reached up and began unpinning the thick swirls of rust red hair from atop her head. "Wanna do dirty stuff, huh? *Real* dirty? Well, I've got a confession to make, too. This is not the first time I've heard a confession like that."

As her hair spilled down across her shoulders, she leaned

forward, running her hands up his thighs from his knees, leaning into him so that he could feel the warmth of her hands through his pants, the weight of her body against him.

"I bet you indeed have heard your share of confessions, Miss Madeleine," Longarm said, trying to keep his wits about him for the moment.

He threw back the rest of his rye and set the glass on an arm of the fainting couch. "Mine is a tad less colorful, however, and I hate to spoil the mood with such tawdry tripe that probably ain't any of my business, anyway."

He leaned forward, took her wrists in his hands, and slid his face to within inches of hers, resisting the urge to close his mouth over those full, rich lips. "But I discovered a half-written note to you in the jailhouse and just can't help wondering who wrote it."

The girl's rust red brows beetled. "To me?"

"My dearest Madeleine," Longarm recited. "Soon, now, you and me shall take our leave of this terrible place."

The girl stared back at him, eyes narrowed slightly.

When she offered nothing, Longarm said, "The note wouldn't be all that curious if I hadn't come across a couple of dead fellas on my way into town earlier. *Hanging* dead fellas. And then, when I got here, the jailhouse was deserted. And it looks as though whoever left hadn't left under exactly the best circumstances."

She smiled as she pushed her head forward and kissed his lips gently. "You know what I think? I think you're just a little overwrought from the bad weather and altitude." She moved her hands to his fly buttons. "I think what you need, to clear your head and settle your stomach, is a blow job."

Longarm's loins rippled and rolled as she undid one button and started on another, her fingers gently jostling his iron-hard shaft. He sucked a breath. "Before you get, uh, all involved down there, Miss Madeleine . . . who over at the jailhouse were you friendly with, if you don't mind me askin'?"

She undid the last button and shoved her hand through the gap, looking up at him coyly from beneath her rust red brows. "Not a soul."

"You don't know who would have written that note?"

"There must be more than one Madeleine in this camp." The girl slid her hand through the fly opening of his long underwear and wrapped her cool, slim fingers around his dong, evoking a shiver of unadulterated pleasure. Her voice was a catlike purr. "Maybe the note was written to someone else."

She continued staring up at Longarm with puppy dog eyes, mouth corners turned up slightly as she slowly, gently slid his cock toward his open fly.

"Any more questions?"

Longarm settled back on the fainting couch, one hand on the arm, the other on the seat beside him, digging his fingers into the rich brocade as his heart leaped with lust. He winced. "I reckon, if there were, they've done escaped me . . ."

She leaned forward and pulled his bulging cock out of his pants, her eyes widening slightly. She groaned and licked her lips with appreciation as she stared down at the meaty organ, then wiggled around on her butt, settling in.

Gripping the shaft by its base with both hands, she touched her tongue to the head. Hot and wet, it sent sparks of desire firing up and down his length, making his stomach leap into his throat.

The girl tongued him for a while, then very slowly slid her mouth over the bulging head and sucked, making wet, crackling sounds beneath the pops and snaps of the wood-stove in the corner and giving Longarm the feeling he was hanging by a thin, frayed rope over a bottomless crevasse.

Back and forth went her head, her full, moist lips caressing him faster and faster, pausing only to run her tongue along the bottom of his shaft and gently nibble his balls.

When he felt his kettle about to boil over, Longarm reached down and grabbed her arms. "Hold on."

Her lips came off his cock with a soft popping sound. She looked up at him with alarm. "Wasn't I . . . ?"

"Take your corset off," he ordered, leaning back to unbuckle his cartridge belt.

She smiled and wiped her mouth with the back of her hand. "Your wish is my command."

He removed his gun and holster, coiling them on the far end of the fainting couch. As he peeled his denims and underwear down his legs, he watched as Madeleine rose and, staring down at him with those brown eyes glistening in the wintry light, undid the strings binding the two flaps of her frilly, pink corset together over her pale, bulging breasts. He kicked out of his boots and pants, then leaned back on the couch to watch her slide the corset flaps back, the pale orbs bulging free, pink nipples pebbling and jutting.

She stepped out of her high-heeled shoes, sat down at the foot of the bed, and began peeling her stockings off. Longarm got out of his shirt and longhandles as fast as he could, then went over and helped the girl with her second stocking.

"Obliged," she said softly, shaking her rich hair from her eyes and leaning back on her elbows. She glanced at the thick bandage encircling his lower torso. "Hurt yourself?"

"Nothin' you can't remedy." Longarm crouched over her, tipping her chin up and closing his mouth over hers.

His cock jutted between his legs, so hard it ached. Kissing him, she snaked one arm around his neck, then reached down and caressed his shaft with her other hand.

When she'd brought him back to boiling, he hauled her up onto the bed, turned her over hastily, and adjusting her smooth, round ass, entered her from behind.

"Ohhh," she sighed as he drove deep to her hot core. "Doggie style." She shuddered as he pulled out and slid back in. "I like that!"

Longarm worked himself into a pasty sweat as, sort of half squatting and half kneeling for maximum support and leverage, he hammered away at the lovely whore for a good fifteen minutes, slowing down occasionally to cool his blood and to prolong the torture.

Once he stopped altogether and climbed off the bed for a pull from the rye bottle. The girl knelt forward atop the bed, hands gripping the slats of the headboard. She bobbed her pretty, sweat-glistening ass in the air and shook her head wildly from side to side, mewling like an angry she-cat, until he climbed back onto the bed and nudged his throbbing, slick organ home once more.

When he came, hammering the headboard against the wall with thunderous reports, the girl fairly screamed, tinkling the lantern sconces and window panes. Still spasming, she dropped to her belly, extended her legs, and twisted onto her back, resting an arm across her flushed forehead.

Longarm leaned down, swept her sweat-damp hair from her face, and kissed her. "You sure know how to satisfy a man, Miss Dominique."

She smiled and smacked her lips, eyes fluttering sleepily. "The pleasure was all mi—"

Her brown eyes snapped wide with shock. Her lower jaw dropped. "H-how did you know?" she rasped.

Longarm grabbed the pillow beside her and, straddling her on his knees, held the pillow up in front of her face.

"Dominique" was embroidered on the end of the pillow case in small, cursive letters.

He dropped the pillow beside her and stared down at her, hooding his eyes gravely. "Where's Madeleine?"

Chapter 11

At the mention of Madeleine's name, Dominique blanched. She wriggled out from under Longarm and sat with her back to the headboard, wrapping her arms around her knees.

"I don't know."

"I don't believe you."

"I don't care if you don't believe me." Dominique's voice was pinched. She looked around the room, nervously running her hands up and down her shins, as if looking for an escape hatch. "Your hour's up. You better leave."

Longarm sat back on his heels, his jaws hard. "Not until you tell me where Madeleine is and why that old whore downstairs made you pretend you were her."

The girl threw him a hard look of her own. "I can't tell you, damnit. I can't tell you anything about anything. Now, if you don't go, I'm gonna scream for Little-Boy." She shook her head, eyes fearful. "Believe me, you don't want to tangle with Little-Boy."

"I'll take my chances with Little-Boy."

Dominique gave a clipped shriek as Longarm grabbed her left leg and pulled her down beside him. He leaned forward on his knees and gritted his teeth as he stared down into her face. "Now, I'm gonna ask you one more time— where's Madeleine and what the hell is going on around here?"

She stared up at him, eyes pinched with fear and fury, tears welling. She opened her mouth but stopped when voices and footsteps rose in the hall. She jerked her head sideways as a gravelly voice said, "You two're in for a real treat. As Ma says, a treat second to none in the whole Territory."

"Little-Boy," the girl whispered as the footsteps grew down the hall to the right of the room, growing as the men approached Dominique's door.

"Second to none, eh?" another voice said, chuckling.

The men passed the door, heavy-soled boots thumping loudly in spite of the floor's carpet runner. Longarm could see their shadows flicker under the door as they passed.

Someone sneezed loudly.

The boot thumps stopped about fifteen feet down the hall to the left of Dominique's room.

Yet another voice, nasal and high-pitched, as though the man had a cold, said, "The camp over to Crystal City has a pretty good little hogpen, too, and I can't believe Miss Sylvania's got anything better . . ."

The man's voice trailed off as someone grunted loudly. There was a clink of iron then a rasping, wooden thud followed by a boom as something heavy hit the floor of the hall. Longarm could feel the vibration through the bed. A creaking, clanking noise rose, followed by another, softer thud.

Longarm stared down at Dominique, who lay with her head turned toward the door. The lawman frowned, ears pricked, puzzled.

"Keeps 'em put away nice, don't she?" one of the men in the hall said, chuckling again.

"Pathway to heaven, boys," Little-Boy said just loudly enough for Longarm to hear. "Yessir, pathway to heaven."

"Shit," one of the others laughed.

The one with the cold sneezed again.

"Uh-uh," Little-Boy grunted. "Lucre first. *Then* heaven."

"In Crystal City, it's heaven first, *then* lucre."

"Fork it over or get the fuck downstairs and quit wasting my time. I got wood to split."

"Jesus H. Christ!" one of the other two exclaimed through a sigh. "This better be the treat you and your ma says it is, or we're gonna demand our money *back*!"

There was a clink of coins followed by the thud of footsteps on creaky stairs. Little-Boy laughed hoarsely—it sounded like a cow coughing. "Hope you both got strong tickers. Remember, you only get an hour."

A wooden clatter and another boom sounded, as of a large door slamming. Little-Boy chuckled, and the ceiling creaked, voices murmuring in the third story above Longarm's head.

In the hall, footsteps grew as Little-Boy approached Dominique's room.

The girl jerked her head toward Longarm with a frightened grunt. She wrapped her arms around his neck, pulling him down to her and pressing her lips to his chest. She groaned loudly as she slid her face around, kissing him, making the bed creak loudly as she rocked her hips.

While the girl squirmed around beneath him, Longarm stared at the crack under the door. A shadow appeared. A few seconds later there was a tap on the door.

"Time's almost up," Little-Boy growled.

The shadow beneath the door disappeared, and Little-Boy's boot thuds drifted off down the hall.

The girl sagged back on the bed with a relieved sigh. "Please go," she said thinly. "And don't let them know you know I'm not Madeleine. They'll blame me."

Longarm climbed off the bed and stepped into his underwear. "What was goin' on out there?"

She didn't say anything, only lay staring up at the ceiling from which footsteps thudded and there was a muffled buzz of conversation.

Grumbling, Longarm moved to the door, opened it a crack, and peered up and down the hall. Finding it empty, he moved out and, drawing the door closed but not latching it, padded barefoot to his left, looking up. He stopped and scrutinized what appeared to be a trapdoor embedded in the high, wainscoted ceiling, with a steel ring in the near end. There were two heavy hinges at the far end.

Judging from the wooden clattering he'd heard when Little-Boy had opened the door, a set of stairs dropped down, allowing access to the third story.

Hearing a man snoring while a girl sang softly in one of the nearby rooms, while bedsprings sang in a room behind him, Longarm stood on the tips of his bare toes and reached for the ring. Even stretching his fingers out as far as they'd go and propping himself practically on the ends of his toenails, his reach was still a good six inches shy of the ring.

He was looking around for a chair when Dominique's door creaked. The redhead peeked out, looking up and down the hall before regarding Longarm with wide-eyed exasperation. "What do you think you're *doing*?" she hissed. "Do you *wanna* die? And get *me* killed, *too*? Get back *in* here!"

Longarm glanced back up at the door beyond which he heard more creaks and sporadic bursts of conversation, several notes of which sounded Chinese. Cursing under his breath, he retreated back into Dominique's room and latched the door quietly behind him.

"They got Chinese girls up there?" Longarm asked the girl. "Is Madeleine up there with 'em?"

Dominique had donned a flannel pink wrapper, and she stood at the dresser, quickly rolling a cigarette with quivering fingers.

"I'm not telling you anything about anything." She didn't look at him as she stuck the quirley between her lips and fired a match on the dresser. "You best leave before Little-Boy comes for you."

"I can take care of Little-Boy." Longarm set his Colt on the dresser and swung the girl around by her shoulders. "I'll make sure he doesn't hurt you. I wanna know what the hell's goin' on around here." He lifted his chin toward the ceiling. "Who's in the attic?"

The girl sucked a deep drag off the quirley and shook her head as she exhaled smoke through her nostrils. She stared straight back at Longarm, her jaw hard, eyes stubborn. "You might—and I say *might*—take care of Little-Boy if you got the drop on him. But this whole town is full of killers, Longarm. And they don't care if you're wearin' a badge. If you get too nosy, you'll disappear and no one will ever hear from you again."

Suddenly, Dominique's upper lip quivered and her eyes glazed with tears as she stared up at him desperately. "Please, get out of here. *Please!* If not for *your* sake, then for *mine*. I have to *live* here!"

"What do you mean, you 'have to'?"

She swung abruptly away, crossing her arms on her chest as she turned to the window.

Longarm wasn't going to get any more out of her. All he'd really gotten out of this whole charade was more questions.

He took another pull from the rye bottle, then pulled his clothes back on as the girl stood smoking and staring out the window. When he'd stomped into his boots and buckled his cartridge belt around his waist, he moved to Dominique still staring out the window, and squeezed her shoulder.

"I'll be back."

As he moved to the door, the girl said thinly behind him, "You'll be in a pine box . . . if you're lucky."

Longarm hesitated at the open door and glanced back at the girl. Then he went out, closed the door, and looked up at the trapdoor in the ceiling once more before turning and tramping off down the hall.

Downstairs, Miss Sylvania Thayer had her wheelchair pulled up to one of the poker tables. Longarm considered requesting a "special" visit to the third story, but he'd only make the woman suspicious and possibly get Dominique in trouble.

He'd have to investigate the third story on his own . . . somewhow.

"So, how was Madeleine?" the old woman said huskily around the long, black cigar wedged in her yellow teeth.

A brunette in a wolf coat was playing the piano, and several more tables were occupied than before, tobacco smoke wafting. The whorehouse had settled jovially in for another day of bad weather.

"Everything I'd heard she would be."

Longarm tossed the woman a coin as he headed for the front door.

On the front porch of Miss Sylvania's House of Ill Repute, Longarm blinked against the heavy snowflakes falling from a gray sky so low that the tops of the peaked roofs across the street were tufted with gauze. Beneath the clouds and behind the slanting snow veil, the log buildings hunched blackly. All he could make out of the high, rocky ridge behind them was a vague, tan shadow.

The whorehouse's porch steps were mantled with a good inch and a half of fresh snow.

Longarm looked around, his thoughts swirling with the snow, frustration picking at him.

Dominique had said the town was full of killers. To Longarm, who hadn't seen any more than fifteen people in the entire town so far, the camp appeared all but abandoned.

He moved out into the street and turned to look back up at the whorehouse as smoke from the building's two stone chimneys mingled in the snowy air above the mansard roof. Four windows faced the street from the third story. The shutters on all four windows were closed.

Who did Sylvania and the big Indian with the unlikely name of Little-Boy have locked up there, anyway? Longarm had almost certainly heard female Chinese voices. Chinese girls were quite the delicacy on the frontier.

Was Madeleine up there, too?

Remembering Mojave Joe, Longarm turned toward the jailhouse at the end of town on the other side of the street, just beyond the general store. He couldn't see much from this distance, but there didn't appear to be any smoke rising from the jailhouse's tin chimney pipe.

Tempting as it was, it wouldn't be professional to let a prisoner freeze to death.

He grumbled as he angled across the street, squinting as the snow caught in his lashes and the icy wind funneled under his buckskin's raised collar. As he passed the general store he turned to see a couple of silhouettes in the windows on both sides of the building's front door. One jerked away quickly, while the other faded slowly from view, as though the man were stepping nonchalantly back into the shadows of the store.

Longarm shot a grin toward the building, pinching his hat brim. Something told him the loafers in the general store were expecting or at least hoping he'd cut and run. They were about to be disappointed.

Even if the weather suddenly cleared, he wouldn't leave Happiness until he found out what the hell was going on.

He pushed through the jailhouse door, stomping snow from his boots. A shadow moved at the back, and Mojave Joe bolted up to his cell door, crouching and holding a wool blanket around his shoulders.

"'Bout time you got back! Fire went out a long time ago!"

Longarm closed the door and moved toward the wood box. "How they hangin', Joe?"

"They don't hang when they're froze off, you son of a cock-suckin' bitch!"

"Careful, Joe, or I'll let you freeze up solid."

"I got rights, you bastard. You can't let me freeze. Now that you got me locked up like a damn dog, you gotta feed and water me and keep me from freezin' my fuckin' prick off!"

Ignoring the prisoner's harangues, Longarm opened the stove's door and shook the ashes down. He added some small sticks to the still-glowing, smoking coals. Gradually, pensively, he added larger logs to the growing fire until the stove was ticking like a steamship's boiler box.

"Now I'll take a cup of coffee and lunch," Mojave Joe ordered.

"Only two meals a day in these digs, Joe." Longarm went to the desk and, staring down at the unfinished note to Madeleine, pulled on his gloves.

"I've been shivering so hard, I'm all hollowed out!" the outlaw protested, gritting his teeth and furiously shaking the cell door, raising a raucous din. "Now feed me or so help me, when I finally get my hands around your thick neck, I'll show no mercy!"

The outlaw paused as Longarm headed toward the door with his rifle. The lawman was still deep in thought.

"Where you goin'?" Joe said, his voice pitched with exasperation.

"Out." Longarm opened the door and glanced back at Mojave Joe staring at him disbelievingly from behind the cell door, each hand wrapped so tight around a bar that his knuckles had turned white as bone. "I'll try to be back to scrounge up your supper, Joe, but I make no promises."

Longarm stepped outside.

Mojave Joe gave the door another fierce jerk. "What if the stove goes out again, you bastard?"

Longarm glanced back through the partly open door. "Then just dwell on the cold grave my friend Buster Davis is lying in down in Alamosa, and be glad you're not in the same condition . . . yet."

He closed the door, turned to the snowy street, lifted his Winchester in both hands, and rammed a fresh shell into the chamber. Then he off-cocked the hammer but kept his right index finger curled through the trigger guard, his thumb on the hammer.

Pressing the rifle's butt against his hip, he moved off to his left, glancing cautiously over his shoulder at the whorehouse and the general store, making sure no one was watching as he headed into the snowy scrub brush and boulders at the west end of town.

Twenty minutes later, covered with enough snow to make him blend easily into the terrain, and having circled wide of the town's west end, he approached the whorehouse from its back side and once again stared up at the third story under the mansard, shake-shingled roof.

As in the front of the place, there were four windows back here. All were shuttered though he spied wan lamplight filtering through cracks in the warped, gray boards. He'd been hoping to find an outside staircase climbing to the third story, but his bad luck was holding.

The only things back here were a two-hole privy, a fresh patch of yellow vomit no doubt left by one of the men from inside, and several wood stacks shrouded with tarpaulins. There was a back door, but Longarm doubted it would do him any good even if it wasn't locked, which, he discovered after gently testing it, it was.

He'd just started moving to investigate the other side of the building when the muffled yaps of coyotes rose in the distance behind the whorehouse—from somewhere in the snowy scrub piñons between the town and the tall ridge just north of it.

Longarm stared toward the din. It sounded like three or four coyotes fighting over carrion.

Remembering that north was the direction from which he'd heard the wolves earlier, he switched course and tramped back into the snow-flocked piñons, meandering around boulders and abandoned miners' shacks, stock pens, wheelbarrows, and sluice boxes.

He followed the yips and growls across a shallow ravine, around a partially mined knoll, and into a wash studded on both sides with snow-laden spruces and tamaracks. He paused beside a sprawling spruce and squinted ahead, where the snow had been kicked up around the base of the wash's right-hand cutbank.

There were several blood splotches and what appeared to be the bones of some animal the coyotes were finishing off after the wolves had no doubt taken most of the meat.

The coyotes themselves—three scrawny, dun blurs—were milling around about fifty yards straight down the wash, between a low, sod-roofed cabin on the left bank and a pine-clad slope on the right. Two of the three coyotes were playing tug-of-war with what appeared to be a hunk of hide.

Longarm started forward, kicking through a drift of snow and hitting something solid, which rolled out ahead of him. He stopped in his tracks and stared down, lower jaw dropping, heart thudding.

The severed head of a beautiful, black-haired woman gaped up at him with empty eye sockets.

Chapter 12

Longarm took one step back from the severed head in horror, oily fingers clenching his gut and nearly making him retch. Looking around wildly, as though the woman's killers might still be lurking, he dropped to a knee, then leaned forward on his rifle, forcing his eyes downward.

He balled his cheeks as he scrutinized the grisly specter before him.

He could tell the woman had been pretty by the delicate shape of her face. Wide cheekbones narrowed to a straight jaw and perfectly rounded chin with a small mole on the side. Her nose was small, mouth narrow, lips full. The long, black hair sprayed out in the snow behind her head, and was now tangled and matted with frozen blood, though he could see it had once been rich and lush.

There was still a trace of paint on her blue white face, and the remnants of a false eyelash clung to the right lid hooding the socket of an eye the magpies and crows had no doubt pecked out a couple of days ago.

Longarm hadn't realized he'd been holding his breath. Now he let it out in a long, raspy sigh, vapor puffing around his face. "Madeleine . . ."

111

He looked around. More human carnage—gnawed bones and clumps of frozen viscera with here and there bits of bloody cloth—pushed up from beneath the freshly fallen snow, having been picked over by the three coyotes still growling and yipping farther up the wash.

Longarm followed the coyotes' scuffed path to the cutbank, part of which had been caved in over the side of the wash—probably over the woman's body, before the wolves and coyotes had dug her up. But then, moving on down the wash and finding several larger bones and a man's bloody, half-gnawed boot, he realized that not only the girl had been discarded here like so much trash.

The body of at least one man was here, as well.

Longarm looked around, kicking through the scrub as the snow fell around him, finding more, larger bones and larger clumps of viscera.

Half-buried in the snow on the leeward side of a spruce sapling, he found a man's hat—a sugarloaf sombrero. He slapped the hat against his thigh, dislodging the snow. A badge was pinned to the tall crown. Longarm held the hat near his eyes and read the word forged into the cheap tin beneath an eagle with spread wings: Town Constable.

"I'll be damned."

Longarm removed the badge, slipped it into his coat pocket, and dropped the hat, which the breeze caught and rolled up against the cutbank. He continued tramping around, scaring off the three coyotes, which headed off yipping, until he was satisfied that the girl and the constable were the only two bodies out here.

Then he retraced his own tracks back to the whorehouse, which he paused to scrutinize once more, trying to figure a way to get into the third story, before heading back in a roundabout way to the jail.

"Back so soon?" said Mojave Joe from his cot as Longarm pushed through the jailhouse's front door. "I ain't froze up solid as a statue yet!"

"You might be soon," the lawman said, opening the stove door to chuck in a few more split logs. "I'll probably be gone a little longer this time."

"No, you won't, damnit. You can't let me freeze to death in here." When Longarm didn't say anything, but only set to work brewing a fresh pot of coffee, Mojave Joe said, "Where the hell you been, anyway? I figured you was just over to the whorehouse playin' hide-'n'-seek with your pecker. What the hell you up to, Longarm?"

"Shut up, Joe," he growled as he filled the coffeepot with water from a cracked stone pitcher, brows ridged with thought.

"Longarm, goddamnit, don't you go sniffin' around for trouble, hear? If you get yourself killed, what the hell would happen to me?"

"Damn, Joe." Longarm sank back in the swivel chair behind the desk as the coffeepot chugged and gurgled atop the stove. "Here, I thought you were just genuinely concerned for my safety."

"It's *my* safety I'm concerned about. Hell, no one even knows I'm here. If you get your fool ass waxed, no one'll find me till spring!"

When the coffee was done, Longarm gave a cup to Joe through the bars on the condition the outlaw kept his mouth shut, then sank bank in the swivel chair and sipped his coffee while he planned his next course of action.

When he'd finished his coffee and refilled Joe's cup— the outlaw was enjoying the belly-wash so much that he'd become as quiet as a church mouse—he fetched an armload of wood for the stove. He stoked the fire, took another

113

couple of swallows of the hot, rich coffee, then buttoned his coat, donned his gloves, and headed back out into the cold and blowing snow.

He took another look up and down the street. He was the only one out. Wincing as a breeze gust chewed at his cheeks still slightly numb from his previous sojourn, he hefted his rifle and tramped back between the jailhouse and the general store to the stable.

Ten minutes later, he'd saddled the coyote dun and was walking the horse through the alley paralleling the main drag, out of view of anyone trying to keep an eye on him. The horse balked at the blowing snow and wind-whipped trash, and Longarm wished he were wearing spurs on his stovepipe cavalry boots.

Finally, after much coaxing, he put the dun into a trot along the snow-covered main trail, heading back in the direction from which he and Mojave Joe had first come. There was some shelter as the trail dropped between rocky walls of spruce, Ponderosa pines, and naked aspens, but the depth of the snow, nearly to the horse's knees in some places, made up for it.

Finally, the two grisly figures swinging from the dead pine appeared in the rocky clearing on a low, windy bench. They were so frosty and snow-covered that he wouldn't have known they were men if he hadn't already seen them. He pulled the dun up to a pine on the opposite side of the trail from the bodies, looked around carefully to make sure he hadn't been followed, then swung down from the cold-stiff leather and tied the reins around a low-slung branch.

The dun shook its head and whinnied, an eerie sound muffled by the wind and sifting snow.

"Easy, fella," Longarm said, patting the horse's hip as he slipped his rifle from the boot. "I just wanna look

114

around a bit, see what I can see. I'll have you back to your stable in no time. Just be glad you ain't stabled with a big-windy like Mojave Joe."

He gave the horse's rump another pat, then, looking around once more, lifted his collar, hefted his rifle, and moved across the trail to the two long figures swinging to and fro in the wind.

The bodies were frozen solid—dark gray specters with black eye sockets stuffed with windblown snow, chins tipped to their chests. The ropes creaked as the wind whistled around the pine bole and swirled the powdery snow around Longarm's boots. The naked cadavers looked so cold there in the knifelike wind that the big lawman jerked with an involuntary shiver.

He swung left of the bodies and began kicking through the drifts piled up around the rocks, shrubs, and small boulders capping the bench around the tree. Beyond, lay what appeared to be glacial rubble that had probably been cracked and sifted by a dozen prospectors.

He moved toward the rubble, tracing a zigzagging path and scrutinizing the uneven ground and layered drifts.

Finding nothing, he stopped and swung farther left, angling back up toward the trail.

He stepped over a fallen tree trunk and stopped, his blood quickening. A triangle-shaped wedge of snow-dusted denim poked up from the snow. He dropped to a knee, leaning on his rifle, and grabbed the cloth. His heartbeat increased as, tugging on a sleeve cuff, an entire jacket rose from the drift, wrinkled and frozen and shedding snow as Longarm shook it and held it out before him.

He gave the jacket a quick inspection, turning it this way and that as the wind nipped at it. Thin and threadbare, the knee-length garment had probably been lying here for a couple of years, no doubt discarded or forgotten by a prospector working the nearby rubble.

Longarm was looking for a badge or anything that might confirm his suspicions that the two hanging men were the constable's deputies. Finding nothing, he dropped the jacket where he'd found it and kicked forward, stumbling over another buried log and almost falling.

A shiver rippled up his back, and he stopped, frowning as he glanced up sharply, looking around warily. The shiver hadn't been caused by the wind pushing against him, but by the feeling he was being watched.

He was raking his gaze from right to left across the gray green woods seventy yards away when four or five crows burst from the trees, their raucous caws tempered by the howling wind. Longarm threw himself right and hit the ground on his shoulder with a grunt as the muffled pop of a rifle sounded amidst the crow calls.

There was another crack slightly to the left of the first report. The bullet plunked into the log he'd stumbled over, blowing up snow and wood slivers. Grunting, he climbed to a knee and raised his rifle, racking a shell. He popped off three quick shots in the direction of the first rifle report.

As he swung the Winchester left, he saw a smoke puff rise from behind a snow-capped boulder, then heard the slug whine past his right ear before spanging off a rock behind him.

A black hat and a red scarf appeared beside the boulder. Taking quick, careful aim, Longarm squeezed the Winchester's trigger once more. The head and scarf snapped back, the man's shrill scream reaching Longarm's ears a half second later.

There were several more cracks as the crows faded against the pine-carpeted ridge to Longarm's right. One slug plunked into the snow six inches from his knee while another sailed high and clipped a tree branch behind him. Spying movement in the corner of his right eye, he turned to see a man running toward him from the base of the forested ridge, holding a rifle across his chest as he ambled through the placer workings.

He was a big hombre in a buffalo coat, his long, black hair falling down from the earflaps of his rabbit hat. Little-Boy.

Longarm triggered a shot at the big Indian, then dropped behind a boulder and looked toward his horse. Another man—a bulky shape amidst the swaying snow veils—moved toward him from that direction, as well, cutting him off from the dun.

He whipped a look over the rocky terrain behind him. Spying no one approaching from that direction, he bolted off his heels and jogged east along the bench as the gray blurs of the two dead cadavers swayed in the wind to his right.

Bullets plunked into the snow-mounded rocks and logs, one burning across the side of his right shin, just above his boot top, evoking a sharp intake of breath through gritted teeth. He spun, emptied his Winchester, then spun again and continued running downslope, leaping the rubble of old placer workings and passing the remains of a roofless miner's shack.

When he dropped beneath the brow of the hill, he hunkered down behind a low tailing pile. He bit off his right glove, then quickly plucked shells from his cartridge belt and thumbed them through the Winchester's loading gate. He was almost finished when two men crested the brow of the hill—one a gray brown shape and the other a black brown shape—straight ahead. The black brown shape yelled something Longarm couldn't hear, and dropped to a knee.

The lawman ducked behind the tailing pile as a slug barked into the pile's other side, spanging shrilly as rock shards and snow flew around him. The rifle's crack sounded little louder than a hiccup beneath the howling wind.

Longarm edged a look over the top of the pile, glimpsed two more figures tracing a zigzagging pattern toward him down the slope, spaced about twenty yards apart. Little-Boy was moving around the hill's far right shoulder, ambling heavy-footed but determinedly over the rocks.

Longarm began to lift the Winchester, but before he could get it leveled, several more slugs ricocheted off the rocks and snow in front of him, driving him back down.

Turning, he looked down the hill falling sharply below his position. He couldn't tell for sure in the shunting snow veils, but it appeared that the slope dropped into a wash or creek bottom, with another forested ridge climbing steeply on the creek's far side.

Lead hammered the tailing pile, the pistols cracking like twigs in the distance.

Longarm cursed. There were about seven men after him, trying to get around him. If they flanked him on the downslope, Billy Vail would soon have a deputy marshal's job to fill.

He waited for a gap in the fusillade, then triggered three quick rounds, hitting little but snow and air but slightly slowing the pace of his pursuers, before wheeling and heading downslope, hopscotching rocks and leaping spruce and piñon saplings.

He could hear the men yelling, heard the rifle cracks and the dull spangs off the snow-mantled rocks. He kept moving, ducking and weaving, his heart pounding, the cold air raking his lungs.

He paused behind a pile of weathered lumber to catch his breath and cast a glance upslope. The seven men were running toward him—vague, bulky shapes spread in a long line from his left to his right. They bounded over rocks and shrubs as they yelled wildly and paused now and then to trigger an errant shot.

Little-Boy, the biggest of the seven, was on the slope's far right side, moving more slowly than the others but deliberately, barking angrily and pausing every few steps to raise his Spencer rifle and trigger a shot from his shoulder.

His long, black hair jostled down from his rabbit hat to brush the shoulders of his buffalo coat, snow billowing out from around his knee-high, fur-trimmed boots.

Longarm ducked behind the lumber to thumb more cartridges into his Winchester. Two slugs slammed into the woodpile with wicked barks, sending up snow puffs. A third sparked off a nail protruding from one of the boards. It ricocheted so close to Longarm's left eye that he could feel the hot wind against his cheek.

Grinding his teeth, he poked his Winchester up, drew a bead on a fast-moving gent in a red hat and green mackinaw, and fired. He heard the *thwack!* as the bullet punched through the man's coat, then the startled grunt as the man, in mid-leap between boulders, dropped his rifle as he continued forward.

He hit the downslope on both feet. His knees buckled and he rolled straight down the slope toward Longarm, piling up against a boulder about twenty feet away, scarlet blood streaking the snow behind him.

"Bastard got Dix!" one of the other pursuers bellowed above the wind as all six closed quickly, the two on each side angling toward the middle of the slope.

Dix was still jerking with death spasms against the boulder as Longarm wheeled and continued bounding downslope, hearing the wind pick up with a roaring rush.

He'd taken only four lunging strides down the steeply pitching slope before his right foot slipped out from under him. He lost the rifle as he fell forward and hit the downslope on his belly and chest.

His breath punched out of his lungs with a giant *Uhffff!*

The slope was icy here as well as steep, and while he dug his boots and arms into the snow, he continued sliding downward, headfirst, skidding along on his chest as though riding a child's sleigh, his chin plowing snow out in front of him.

What he could see through the snow he didn't like a bit.

With a sickening clench of his gut, he saw that it wasn't the wind he'd heard. The whooshing sound was the watery roar of an ice-fringed creek angling along the base of the slope, churning and frothing as it tumbled downhill. The stream grew in front of Longarm by leaps and bounds, hurling his stomach into his throat and turning his loins to jelly.

Desperately he pounded the ground with his boots and fists . . . to no avail.

He continued hurtling virtually straight down the slope, his rifle bouncing along ahead and to his left.

"Sheee-ittttt!"

He had to get stopped or he'd drop right into that near-frozen, churning, broiling stream.

He hadn't finished the thought before he did just that.

Chapter 13

Longarm hit the water nose first, plunging through a lacy film of ice and barreling deep into the stream's frigid depths.

The water was so cold that, for a half second as his momentum propelled him straight down to the stream's rocky bottom—fortunately the water was a good eight or nine feet deep along this section—it almost felt scalding. But then, as he pushed with his gloved hands off the bottom and angled back toward the surface, the cold felt like a million tiny chisels chipping away at every bone in his body.

His heart and lungs shriveled. His eyes receded into their sockets. His ears rang.

"Pooo-ahh!" he grunted as his head broke the surface, spitting water and sucking a breath while feeling the iron hand of the stream's current push, pull, and twist him downstream.

Gulping air, he swiped at the water's frothing surface, trying to fight his way to the right bank. It was like trying to run against a Kansas cyclone. The current held him tight in a fickle grip and shepherded him downstream as though he were no more than a stick of driftwood.

The rocky, ice- and snow-flocked banks swept by in a blur and he stopped fighting for anything but to keep his head above water. Several times the stream threw him against rocks to which he tried to cling, but his gloved hands slid off the snowy stone without so much as slowing him down. Beneath him, submerged rocks reached up to bark against his shins and thighs.

The cold water seemed to permeate his every fiber. As the water careened down the quickly dropping canyon, he felt as though his blood were turning to jelly, his brain to cork. His vision dimmed and his breath grew shallow.

A nearly inaudible voice deep inside his head told him that, as quickly as he was bounding downstream, pirouetting like a dancing bear with his arms and legs flailing at the water, he was freezing to death.

The stream was relentless. On and on it swept him, throwing him over short falls and propelling him through riffles and narrow channels between half-submerged boulders. He heard himself grunting and yelling, his exclamations echoing off the rocky banks, but the sounds seemed to emanate from someone else far away.

Finally, the river slowed and widened, fanning out in a broader, shallower bed, with tall pines pushing up on both sides, iron gray behind the slanting snow. Longarm's legs were so numb that he only vaguely felt his boots skimming along the bottom before the water level dropped sharply and he found himself kneeling, half-floating on the bottom, the current only nudging him now, not propelling him like before.

Shivering uncontrollably, he crawled along the creek bed, the chill water swirling around him. He gained the shallows, where snow-tufted cattails grew, then pushed through the reeds to the shore. His entire body ached from the cold, as though his nerves were lying outside his skin, and with every movement as he crawled up the gravelly shore amidst the pines, he grimaced and winced and cursed under his breath.

"Bl-blood's . . . gonna freeze . . . up-up . . . solid . . . if I don't get a fire goin' . . . get d-dry."

He stopped crawling when his boots were clear of the stream, and rolled onto his back, crossing his arms on his chest. His body shook as though he were sprawled in the box of a wagon moving fast over rocky ground.

"Can . . . can't lay here. Gotta . . . get a . . . f-f-fire goin' *g-g-g-g-goddamnit*!"

Something appeared in the upper periphery of his vision as he stared at the gauzy sky through the snow-glazed pine boughs surrounding him. It was oval-shaped. He blinked. His mind worked so slowly that it took him several seconds to realize that a face was staring down at him from beneath a deerskin hat with a rabbit-fur brim.

"Who're you?" the man grumbled.

His face was silhouetted against the sky, but Longarm could tell that he was old—probably in his seventies—and that he was bearded. The leathery skin above the bridge of his nose wrinkled with curiosity, as though Longarm were some strange fish that had washed up out of the stream and the man was merely wondering if he were edible.

Longarm tried to form words—he wanted the man to build him a fire, pronto—but his teeth only clattered together as he grunted and groaned.

The oldster glanced to his right. "Hey, Mel, come over here. Lookee what I found."

Soft-soled boots crunched snow, and another head moved into Longarm's field of vision, staring down at him. This man was taller. He was also bearded, though his beard didn't show as much gray as the first man's, and he wore a heavy coonskin cap and black leather patch over his right eye.

He chuffed with bemusement. "What in the name of flaming dog shit are you doin' out here, amigo?"

Longarm stared up at the man. *"F-f-f-f-fire!"*

The shorter, older man frowned at the taller man. "He was escapin' a fire?"

The taller man with the eye patch shrugged. He wore a four-point capote with red and black stripes and a black stocking cap. His face was sharp-featured and long-nosed, with a jutting, bearded chin. Long, gray black hair hung to his shoulders.

"I reckon he expects us to build him one."

"Probably one o' them snakes from Happiness." The older man lowered the barrel of an old Spencer carbine toward Longarm's head. "I'll put him down and throw him back in the creek."

"Hold on." The taller man handed the shorter man his own rifle—a Winchester Yellowboy repeater—and squatted beside Longarm.

"F-f-fire," Longarm mumbled. "Fr-free-zin' . . . m-m-m-my *ass off*!"

"Hold on, amigo," the taller gent said. "Just gonna see what you got on ya." He chuckled. "Any gamblin' winnings?"

Most of Longarm's coat buttons had come undone in the creek. The tall man opened the remaining two and spread the flaps away from his chest.

The tall man whistled when he saw the badge on Longarm's left breast, just above his shirt pocket. "Now, lookee there. Got us a *lawman*!"

"Holy shit!" intoned the older gent, leaping back as

124

though from a coiled rattlesnake. "Get back, Mel. I'll drill him!"

As the older gent cocked his rifle loudly, the taller man shoved the barrel aside with his fur-mittened hand. "Hold on, Alvin. We ain't gonna kill no lawman."

"But Mel . . ."

"Statute o' limitations done run out on your crimes twenty years ago, you old fool. Now step down and put that long gun away. If this man really is an officer of the law"—he shuttled his glance back to Longarm still shivering on the ground before them—"then it's my duty as a former toter of the badge my ownself to render aid."

He shook his head as he ran his gaze up and down Longarm's soaked, quivering frame. "Damn, son, you don't look a *bit* good. How long were you out there, anyway?"

"F-f-f-fire, f-f-f-fer chri-chri-chris-sakes!"

"All right, all right," Mel said. "Don't be so impatient." He glanced at the older gent. "Alvin, why don't you high-tail it back to the cabin and build up the fire? Take my rifle. I'll see if I can throw this big, wet bastard over my back."

"What about huntin'?"

"We got enough meat for tonight. We'll hunt tomorrow."

Alvin gave Longarm a wary, sidelong glance, muttering inside his beard, then turned and hoofed it into the trees.

"Come on, sport." Mel leaned down, grabbed the lawman's left arm, and pulled him up over his shoulder, grunting again as he straightened his legs and Longarm's weight settled on his back. Longarm coughed as, hanging upside down against the man's broad back, water gurgled up from deep in his lungs.

Mel turned and Longarm watched his boots kick snow as he followed Alvin's tracks into the woods. Longarm's teeth continued clicking together. The knife wound in his back throbbed. Beyond that, he couldn't feel much of anything anymore except a dull ache in every joint. His heart was slowing and the snow behind Mel's boots grew steadily darker, as though the sun were going down.

Then the snow turned black as April mud in a mining camp's main street, and the crunch of Mel's boots faded to silence.

Longarm was only vaguely aware of time passing and of intermittent, indistinct sounds around him before he suddenly smelled pine smoke and roasting meat and felt heat—sweet, soothing heat—engulfing him.

He opened his eyes, turned toward the source of the warmth. Orange flames leaped in a broad, stone hearth around split, mounded logs only four or five feet away. There were voices around him, and occasional laughter and the ticking of cards being slapped down on a table, but Longarm's head weighed too much to turn it again, and once again, his lids grew heavy.

They closed down over his eyes once more, and sleep engulfed him.

Something nudged his left shoulder. He growled, annoyed, sleep holding him. The nudge came again and a gruff voice said, "Come on, lawdog. Best have you a bite."

Longarm smelled meat wafting on warm steam. He opened his eyes, blinking groggily, and looked around at the log walls on which antlers and hides were hung. Bright sunlight pushed through two windows, one on each side of a heavy, timbered door.

To his right, a fire popped, spreading smoky warmth around him. To his left, a big, black-haired man with an eye patch stared down at him, holding a speckled blue cup in one hand, a spoon in the other. Meat and gravy were mounded atop the spoon, steaming. Longarm's belly grumbled. It was so empty that his ribs seemed to be pressing against his backbone.

Longarm began to lift his right hand, but his arm was so weak he couldn't get it above the heavy buffalo robe pressing him into the floor.

"Open up. I'll shovel her in," said the big man with the eye patch.

Longarm did as he was told, staring up at the man—Mel something-or-other. Longarm's brain was still sluggish. His limbs beneath the robes felt rubbery, his fingers and toes prickling. .

Mel slid the spoon between his lips. Venison stew with potatoes and carrots. Longarm had never tasted food so good. His stomach rumbled eagerly as Mel spooned another load into his mouth. While he could feel the soothing, strengthening nourishment almost instantly, after the fourth or fifth spoonful, he began to feel slightly nauseated, and he waved the man off.

"Obliged."

"You been empty for a couple days, Mr. uh . . ."

"Custis Long," he grumbled. "Folks call me Longarm."

"Heard of ye, matter o' fact," Mel said with a nod. "Prob'ly gonna take your stomach time to get used to grub again, Longarm."

"No doubt it—" Longarm stopped, frowning, then jerked his head up so quickly that the room spun around him. He blinked, cleared his throat. "Did you say *days*?"

"This is your third one here. I gave you some deer broth yesterday, and a couple spoonfuls of whiskey. Otherwise, you've been over here sawin' logs while Alvin and me been out huntin' and splittin' wood, tryin' to keep that fire goin'." Mel glanced toward the door. "Colder'n a grave digger's ass out there."

Longarm closed his eyes, thinking hard, remembering. He'd locked up Mojave in the jailhouse in Happiness. The jailhouse stove had gone out a long time ago. If no one had stoked it, the outlaw was no doubt frozen up tauter than a two-by-four.

"Shit."

"What's wrong?"

Longarm gave a grunt as he flipped back a corner of the buffalo robe, vaguely aware of a fresh bandage wrapped about his lower torso, padding the knife wound. "I gotta get back to Happiness." He moved his legs, tried to stand, but the room spun around him faster than before. He sank back against the grass-stuffed burlap sack he'd been using for a pillow, feeling weak as a feather in a heavy wind.

Someone chuckled behind Mel, and Longarm heard a raspy, high-pitched voice. "You ain't goin' nowhere for at least a couple days, badge toter. Judging by the three or four goose eggs on your head, that creek done bounced you off a couple o' good-sized rocks. Didn't do that knife wound any good, either."

There was a raspy laugh, and Longarm glanced behind Mel to see the old, gray-bearded gent, Alvin, sitting in an elkhorn rocker and darning a pair of socks. The old man's bare feet were sunk in a pan of steaming water, his buckskin trousers rolled halfway up his pale, bony shins.

"Tell ya the truth, I can't believe you're still kickin'," the oldster added. "I done bet Mel a thimbleful of gold dust we'd be tossin' your carcass to the wolves by yesterday noon!" He shook his head as he continued to darn, rock, and soak his feet. "That's at least two bottles of good hooch I'm out, damn ye . . ."

Longarm kneaded his forehead as he regarded his gear—clothes, coat, and gun belt—hanging off a hide-bottomed chair angled toward the fire. His clothes had long since dried, his denims and longhandles hanging stiffly down from beneath his coat.

He was surprised to see his .44 in its holster. He vaguely remembered seeing his Winchester splash into the river ahead of him—lost forever.

"I'll pay you back as soon as I get back to town," Longarm told Alvin.

"Happiness?" Mel had taken the stew back into the kitchen on the opposite side of the cabin—little more than a square table, a couple of chairs, a counter constructed of two long planks, and a half dozen cluttered shelves. "Best steer wide of that perdition." Holding a brown bottle, he turned toward Longarm. "How'd you end up in the creek?"

"Let me guess," said Alvin, pushing his long, threaded needle through a heavy gray sock with a caustic chuff. "Stayed in Happiness *too damn long*."

"Give the man a cigar," Longarm said, relaxing against the pillow and the bobcat hide beneath him. "But I gotta tend my prisoner—if I still have one—and settle up with the men who hoorawed me into that creek." He glanced at Mel, who approached holding another tin cup. "You fellas know a big Indian named Little-Boy?"

"Of course," both men said at once. Mel extended the cup to Longarm. "Have a shot of tanglefoot. Best medicine on God's green earth. Alvin makes it in a tub out to the stable, and he swears he don't add the strychnine nor the snake heads they say Little-Boy's ma, Miss Sylvania, adds to hers, but Alvin's a liar from way back."

Alvin chuckled, then snapped a curse as he poked himself with his needle.

Longarm took the sharp-smelling cup and scowled up at Mel, incredulous. "Little-Boy's Miss Sylvania's *son*?"

"You got it," Mel said, easing his big frame into a chair with a heavy sigh. "Had her a Comanche husband till he got shot in some saloon down Texas-way. Her and Little-Boy made their way north, with her whorin', till she'd earned enough to open her own brothel in Alamosa. She ran the Purple Palace for nigh on eight years before the Happiness camp opened, and she hauled her setup and Little-Boy up there and *really* started raking it in! She went far and wide to find the best whores on the frontier." Mel held his cup out toward Longarm for emphasis, squinting his lone eye over the rim. "And once she got 'em, she didn't let 'em go, neither. Not ever!"

Alvin was threading another needle, hipped around in his chair for the bright sunshine pushing through the sashed window behind him. "They say Miss Sylvania's whores only leave feet first, and havin' resided in Happiness a few years my ownself, I can tell you that it's a bonded fact. *Ouch! Goddamnit!*"

"She caught one of her girls trying to escape," Mel said. He'd hiked a fur-trimmed moccasin boot on his knee and was rolling a smoke. "The girl stabbed her in the back, crippled her. Little-Boy took the girl into the main street of Happiness and whipped her to death with a blacksnake. One of the other girls objected, so he dragged her out and gave *her* the same medicine."

"They're quite a pair," Longarm growled, sipping the hooch. It burned his throat like turpentine but sent a pleasant flush through his body.

"What'd you do to get 'em on your case?" Mel said. "Cheat at cards, did ya? Or maybe you bruised one of her Chinks. No one bruises Miss Sylvania's Chinks, don't ya know!"

Chapter 14

Longarm had just taken another sip of the whiskey. At Alvin's mention of "Chink," he swallowed wrong. Pulling the cup down, he choked and turned teary eyes on the old man darning socks in his rocker while his feet soaked in the steaming tub on the floor.

"So there *are* Chinese!"

"Five, last I heard," Mel said. "Good-lookin' girls straight from the slave trade in San Francisco. Never seen 'em myself. Shameful, if you ask me."

"Last time I made a supply run to Happiness, I heard one of 'em hanged herself with her own robe," said Alvin. He clucked and shook his head sadly as he began mending a tear on the shoulder seam of a sheepskin vest. "Shameful is right. Plenty enough girls *wanna* hire out. No point in forcin' girls that don't. Must be a sin somewhere in the Good Book, fer certain sure."

"Why does she do it?" Longarm asked.

"Big money in Chink girls," Mel said, adjusting his eye patch and blowing smoke at the rafters. "She can make four, five times more on a Chink than she can on a white girl or even a mulatto. Most of the other business men in town back

131

her play, seein' as how having Chinese whores—especially *young, good-lookin'* Chinese whores—keeps more men in the camp every winter, and when word gets around, it brings more men *back* in the spring."

Longarm tapped his cup thoughtfully, letting the information sort itself out in his still-foggy brain.

He glanced at Mel. "What about Madeleine?"

"What about her?"

"She worked for Miss Sylvania, I take it."

"Sure 'nough," Alvin chuckled. "Best-lookin' whore in many a mile. French, too." He glanced at Mel, who laughed lustily and took another deep drag off his quirley.

"I got a feelin' Madeleine's dead," Longarm said. "In fact, I think I stumbled on her in the ravine behind the whorehouse. Along with the body of the town constable."

"Shit you say!" Alvin said, lifting both feet out of the steaming tub with a splash. "That bitch killed *Madeleine*?"

Longarm hiked a shoulder. "Long black hair? Little mole about right here?" He touched the side of his chin.

Alvin nodded, making a face inside his shaggy, gray beard.

Longarm shuttled his gaze between the two men, squinting at a sudden throbbing at the back of his neck. "Did the constable have a couple of deputies? One who might have been in love with Madeleine?"

"Not last time I was in town," Alvin said. "That was a couple months ago, now."

"Could be," Mel said. "Kermit Ervin, the constable, was a God-fearin' man. He might've decided to shut Miss Sylvania down and hire himself some help. Why do you ask?"

Longarm told them about the two men hanging from the tree, and about Little-Boy's gang jumping him while he rode out for a more thorough investigation.

132

"Shit," Alvin muttered. "Sounds like things is heatin' up over to Happiness!"

"Not Mojave Joe," Longarm growled, throwing the last of his hooch back. His brain ached not only from the cold water and the beating against the rocks. He was badly confused. He had to get back to Happiness and start setting things right, whatever that entailed. But at the moment, he was in no condition to do anything but sleep.

The cup dropped from his fingers, and his heavy lids closed with a sound inside his head like that of a door slamming.

When he woke again, he was surprised to find it was only early evening of the same day. He rose and, feeling stronger, sat at the supper table with Mel Marshal and Alvin Henin. He wolfed down two big bowls of venison stew and two thick wedges of Alvin's crusty, whole-wheat bread slathered in gravy, then stayed up to play a couple hands of blackjack for matchsticks while a popping fire held the chill, starry night at bay beyond the frosty windows.

When fatigue began weighing on him once more, he threw in his cards and pushed back his chair. "Much obliged for your hospitality, gents," he said, hauling himself to his feet. He wore only his longhandles and wool socks. "I'll be headin' out first thing in the mornin'. Since I lost my Winchester in the river, I'd be extra obliged if I could borrow one of your long guns, and a sheathed knife for backup. I'll have Uncle Sam settle up with you just as soon as I get back to Denver."

"Don't mean to tell you your job, Longarm," Alvin said over the brim of his steaming coffee mug, which was liberally spiced with whiskey, "but you best head straight back to Denver and fetch yourself some backup. Happiness ain't the happy camp it once was. It's full of killers on the roll of Little-Boy and his ma. And them who ain't trained killers is all businessmen who see that House of Ill Repute as their diamond in the cow pie, if you get my drift. None of them would be against back-shootin' a lawman—federal or otherwise—either!"

"I appreciate the warning, Alvin," Longarm said, stretching one arm above his head while scratching his chest with his other hand. "But that'd take too long. I intend to free those girls from that crazy woman's third floor and settle up my own bill with Little-Boy." He turned and ambled off to his hides and quilts piled in front of the fire. "G'night, and thanks again."

Mel Marshal, who'd once been sheriff of a small town in western Kansas before the gold fever had lured him west, stubbed out a cigar in a tin cup. "You're a stubborn man, Custis. But if you're gonna walk alone into that baili-wick, I'd admire for you to take that Henry rifle hanging over the door. I'll set out my old bowie knife for ya first thing in the morning." He squinted his lone eye at Longarm snuggling down in his bed, and said with a tone of barely controlled rage, "And I hope you bury the blade to the hilt in that big Indian's fat belly!"

Longarm lifted his head from his pillow, frowning across the room at the burly ex-lawman with the sharp face and dark, brooding eye. "Got some history with Little-Boy, do ya, Mel?"

"Little-Boy's the reason I'm wearin' this eye patch." Flushing angrily, Mel took another pull from his whiskey-laced coffee and squeezed a big, brown hand around his playing cards. "I wasn't in the country long when him and me had a run-in outside Happiness late one summer night, after I won over two hundred dollars playin' blackjack at his ma's place.

"He claimed I was cheatin', and him and three other bruisers put the hurt on me real good with hickory ax handles. I woke up with my winnin's gone and my eye dangling halfway down my cheek. I'd have taken my revenge on Little-Boy a long time ago . . . if it weren't for them other killers workin' for him and his dear sweet ma. If they don't want you in Happiness, you won't be in Happiness. Not long, anyways. Much less in Miss Sylvania's House of Ill Repute."

Longarm sagged back against his pillow and stared pensively up at the ceiling. Finally, he loosed a deep sigh. "I hope I can put that knife to good use for you, Mel." He didn't like the doubt he heard in his own voice. "I truly do."

He closed his eyes and didn't wake up when Alvin banked the fire beside him and the two prospectors climbed the ladder to their cots in the cabin's loft. He didn't awaken to anyone stoking the fire during the night, either, but someone must have, for when he woke at the first wash of gray light against the windows, the fire was flaming over several charred logs.

At the same time he hauled his rested but still bruised and battered body up from the hides and quilts, the two prospectors were stirring in the loft, hacking and coughing and splashing water into basins for morning sponge baths. Alvin came down first and started breakfast. Mel followed a few minutes later. After Longarm had given himself a whore's bath at the kitchen tub, he and Mel sat at the rough-hewn table in stony silence, smoking and drinking coffee while flapjacks and bacon popped and sizzled atop the stout iron range. Alvin danced around, cooking and humming with a pensive air.

No one said anything by way of conversation until Longarm swabbed his plate with the last bite of pancake, threw back the last of his coffee, and rose.

"Well, I reckon I'll be pullin' my picket pin, fellas." He grabbed a sheathed bowie knife off a chair by the door, crouched down, and jerked his denim cuffs above his boot tops. "If I'm still kickin' tomorrow, I'll return your weapons."

"Hold on, Custis." Mel stubbed out his cigarette and reached for the old Winchester leaning against the wall beside him. "I'm goin' with you."

Longarm looked at the big, dark, broad-shouldered man as he tied the bowie sheath to his calf with a neckerchief. "I appreciate the offer, but—"

"It ain't no offer," Mel said as Alvin closed the damper on the kitchen range. "I got to thinkin' overnight—I can't let you ride into that bailiwick alone. Not when I got a score to settle my ownself with Little-Boy. Besides, I once wore a badge, even if it was just a deputy sheriff's tin star carved out of a peach can lid. That makes us pards in a way."

"I reckon I'm goin', too," Alvin said, heaving a sigh as he grabbed a soft-leather cartridge belt off a coat hook and wrapped it around his paunchy waist. From the holster jutted the worn grips of an old Colt Navy. "Wouldn't be right—me sittin' here playin' solitaire while my partner's out tradin' lead with Little-Boy's curly wolves." He glanced at Mel, blue eyes flashing uncertainly. "It *wouldn't* be right, would it?"

"You stay, Alvin," Mel said. "You're too old and stove up for gunplay."

"Damn your eyes, that ties it!" Alvin bellowed, red-faced, grabbing his quilted deerskin coat off another wall hook. "I'm goin'!"

Longarm shrugged into his own coat as Mel did the same. "You both stay. Three against a whole camp isn't a whole lot better odds than one. But kidnapping and slavery—not to mention the killing of lawmen—is a federal crime, so it's my job to try to spring those girls."

"Don't worry, Custis," Mel said, spreading his lips with an oblique grin. "I wouldn't be volunteering my services if I didn't think we had a chance."

Longarm grabbed the Henry repeater from the two nails above the door and frowned at the one-eyed former deputy sheriff. "What makes you think we have a chance?"

Mel gave Alvin a conspiratorial glance, then moved around Longarm and opened the door. "Follow me."

As Mel went out into the chill dawn air, Longarm glanced at Alvin, who'd just donned his coat and was tying the ear flaps of his rabbit hat beneath his chin. The gray-beard shrugged. "I don't know what the hell he's got up his sleeve. He never tells me nothin', just gives orders. Worse than a damn woman!"

Longarm worked the Henry's cocking mechanism, making sure the sixteen-shot repeater was loaded, then headed out the door. With Alvin close on his heels, he followed Mel's large, dark figure around the cabin.

A log, brush-roofed stable hunkered in the pines and boulders at the base of a low, forested ridge. Behind it, a frozen creek angled through snow-flocked shrubs.

Left of the stable was a large corral strewn with fresh hay. Four stout mules hung their heads over the corral fence, staring toward the approaching men and blinking their big eyes expectantly, one dropping steaming plop into the trampled snow behind him. Another brayed, and that set the others off, so that as Mel opened the two broad doors on the stable's right side, all four mules worked themselves into a raucous chorus.

Longarm and Alvin followed Mel into the stable's dark interior rife with the smell of straw, leather, and mule shit. Mel led them to the back, near the grain bins, and set his boot on a four-by-four-foot plank box with a rusty padlock.

"If you're fixin' to waltz into Miss Sylvania's place and spring them slanty-eyes, you're gonna need one hell of a diversion. And I got just the thing."

Mel dropped to a knee, then felt around between the unchinked logs behind the locked box, producing a key. He used the key to open the lock and threw open the lid.

The wan gray light seeping between the unchinked logs revealed a good twenty or thirty dynamite sticks resting in a bed of crushed hay, like giant cigars snugged down in a rich man's humidor. Caps and fuses resided at the box's right end.

Alvin chuckled.

Longarm whistled as he dropped to a knee beside Mel. He plucked one of the sticks from the box, raised it to his nose, and sniffed.

"Well, I'll be damned," he said. He looked at Mel. "We could blow up all of Happiness with just half of what you have here!"

Chapter 15

Longarm had expected to walk to Happiness, following the stream back the way he'd come. But since the prospectors had the mules, he soon found himself on a big pinto gelding plowing with ease through the freshly sculpted drifts.

The air was mild compared to how it had been—probably around twenty, twenty-five degrees, Longarm judged—but the sky was low and gray, again threatening snow.

Mel led the way toward Happiness from the southeast, following an old prospector's wagon trace on a heavy-hipped cream mare. Alvin followed Longarm astraddle a mulish gray, which he cursed loudly when, about every ten yards, the beast tried to wheel and bolt back to the warmth of its stable.

In the saddlebags draped across the rump of each mule the men each carried five sticks of dynamite—more than enough, Longarm figured, to create an adequate diversion while he squirreled the Chinese girls from Miss Sylvania Thayer's forbidden third floor. Just how the diversion would be effected, he had no idea. He hoped something came to him by the time they got to town.

"We should've waited till after dark to ride in there," Alvin said as they climbed a low, pine-stippled rise, heading toward the saddleback ridge. "Little-Boy might figure you died in that creek, Longarm. But, then again, he and his boys might be keepin' an eye out for ya, just in case you turned out to be the lucky son of a bitch you did in fact turn out to be!"

The oldster chuckled hoarsely, gigging the stubborn gray around a sharp trail bend.

"It'd be easier to get into town," Longarm allowed, swaying the pinto's easy stride. "But harder to get out with three girls. And I 'spect the temperature'll drop about twenty degrees after dark. Don't really want to rescue those Chinese just to have 'em freeze to death."

"Reckon you gotta point there." Alvin raised his voice so Mel could hear. "Also reckon this is the craziest damn stunt I ever pulled in my life, and I deserve to get my ass greased for playin' along with this foolishness."

"Why don't you let that mule turn and haul your scrawny ass *home*?" Mel called from the head of the pack.

"Why don't you shut up and ride?" Alvin retorted. "I'll give ole Ernie his head when I'm good and ready!"

The graybeard continued cursing under his breath, batting his heels against the mule's ribs.

Longarm smiled to himself as, removing a glove, he dug in his shirt pocket for a cigar, which he'd also borrowed from the prospectors. Coincidentally, they happened to be the three-for-a-nickel variety he himself favored.

He smoked the cigar as they followed the winding wagon trail, which the wind had cleared of snow in places, up a long rise through boulders and spruces in which chickadees and waxwings chittered and sang and squirrels argued. He'd drawn the cigar down to a two-inch stub by the time they crested the saddleback rise and brought Happiness into view on the other side.

Quickly, before they could be spotted from below, they pulled the mules off the trail and into a gap in the boulder-strewn ridge crest.

Longarm shucked the Henry rifle from the saddle boot, then hunkered down in a gap between boulders, staring down the long, easy grade spotted with boulders, mine rubble, and prospectors' log or dugout cabins, most of which pushed up from the snow like oversized gravestones, appearing abandoned.

A good three hundred yards away, at the bottom of the valley, Happiness nestled—little more than two slate-colored, parallel lines from this distance, smoke wisping from chimneys. Two brown dots moved along the street, horseback riders heading in opposite directions.

Several horses stood before the tall log building Longarm took to be Miss Sylvania's House of Ill Repute. He could barely make out the jailhouse, either, and wondered whether Mojave Joe was still kicking or if he'd froze up like a cat in a Dakota blizzard.

Somewhere unseen on the other side of the business district, a dog barked, the sounds small but clear in the still air in which occasional snow flurries danced and fell. The barks were the only sound, and the two riders were the only movement.

No, the barks weren't the only sound. So faint as to be almost inaudible, Longarm could intermittently hear the faint tinkling of a piano.

"Your dance, Custis," Mel said, crouching and holding his Winchester off Longarm's right shoulder. Alvin hunkered down on the other side of Mel, blue eyes reflecting the gray light as he stared down at the town and nibbled his soup-strainer mustache. Mel glanced at Longarm. "How you wanna call it?"

Longarm swept his steely gaze back and forth along the town, beneath the brim of the knit cap with which Louis had supplied him. He'd lost his Stetson along with his rifle in the river.

"That livery barn on the east end of town," Longarm said. "Anyone run it this time of year?"

"The San Antone? Nah." Mel jerked his head left. "The only livery open in the winter is the Johnson Federated just west of Miss Sylvania's."

"How 'bout we blow it up?"

"The San Antone?"

"If no one's in it—and no horses are in it—let's blow the son of a bitch to Kingdom Come. I hate to destroy an innocent man's property, but we're gonna have to blow up something to empty out that whorehouse. With the hay that's no doubt in the livery barn, it'll burn brighter than hell on Saturday night."

Mel brushed a gloved finger across his long, pitted nose. "Shit, a fire that size'll spread fast."

"That's what I'm hopin'. It'll threaten the whole town, and keep everyone well distracted from the whorehouse. Hell, Miss Sylvania'll probably wheel herself out there to haul water up from the creek."

Alvin wheezed a laugh. "Hell, Horace Hanson runs the San Antone."

Longarm glanced at the old graybeard, one eyebrow arched.

"Horace likes to visit the Chinese girls," Mel explained. "It's sort of a joke—him bein' as big and fat as he is, and him favorin' them little slanty-eyes."

Longarm spat to one side. "Sounds like just the man to

142

pick on." He began tramping back toward the mules. "Let's mosey down and start the shindig."

Longarm and the two prospectors led the mules down the slope, tracing a meandering course around ore piles and miners' huts and keeping a sharp eye out for Little-Boy's armed thugs. Longarm figured Little-Boy thought he was dead, but like Alvin had warned, he might keep a couple of men out and about town, just in case the federal deputy returned.

They approached the rear of the buildings lining the south side of the main street and, avoiding trash piles and privies, began making their way east along the alley. They'd moved maybe thirty yards, hurrying past the gaps between buildings, when something large and black rose suddenly on Longarm's right. He jerked with a start, dropping the mule's reins and raising the Henry.

He held fire as the mass of crows and magpies careened off, screeching from the roof of a chicken coop sheathed in snowy brush, wings lifting a loud whooshing noise.

Longarm lowered the Henry. With a relieved sigh, he glanced behind at Mel and Alvin, both of whom looked like someone had just stepped on their graves. Then he retrieved the mule's reins and continued leading the beast eastward.

As they approached the livery barn's rear corral, built from unpeeled pine logs, the corral itself layered with untrammeled, virgin snow, Longarm tied the pinto mule's reins to the top corral pole.

He turned to Mel and Alvin leading their own mules up behind him. "Either of you boys have a timepiece?"

"Of course," Alvin groused. "We ain't *completely* backward."

Longarm retrieved the five sticks of dynamite from his saddlebags and extended two of the sticks to Mel. "Give me exactly one hour. I wanna be *inside* the brothel when you blow the barn, so I have plenty of time to get the girls out. That fire'll no doubt spread like news of a preacher's indiscretions with the schoolmarm."

He held up his own three dynamite sticks. "I'm gonna use these to blow the brothel once I get all the girls outside."

"Just how in the hell are you gonna get *in* there, Custis?" Mel said, a furry black brow hooding his lone eye. "Just waltz in the front door and say 'Hidy-ho, I'm back'?"

Alvin chuffed. "They'll grease you where you stand!"

"I'm gonna go in disguise." Longarm handed Alvin his dynamite sticks, then began unbuttoning his mackinaw. "Mel, you're about my size. Give me your coat and hat."

Mel glanced at Alvin, who, holding Longarm's dynamite a good two feet out away from him, shrugged. Mel chuckled, then began unbuttoning his three-point capote. "You're gonna need more than that."

"I'll walk with a limp and take my chances."

When the men had exchanged coats and hats, Longarm pulling Mel's coonskin cap down low over his eyes, Longarm reached for his Henry.

"Hold on." Mel slipped his eye patch off his head, laying bare the grizzled, empty socket. "Take this. I reckon I could be eight feet tall with a donkey dick draggin' along the ground between my legs, and all anyone would really notice is the eye patch!"

Frowning reluctantly, Longarm slowly extended his hand toward the patch dangling before him.

Mel jerked the patch at him. "Go on! It don't bite. I guarantee it'll get you over the threshold. Now, whether or not it'll keep ya there is a whole other problem."

Longarm took the patch, slipped the rawhide cord over his head, but left the patch a couple of inches above his right eye. He'd pull it down when he needed it.

"Obliged." He grabbed the Henry and canted his head toward the pinto. "Take my mule. When you blow the barn, hightail it with all three mules back the way we came, around the east end of town. Wait for me in the alley behind the whorehouse, but stay out of sight till you see me. I'm gonna try to sneak those girls out the back."

Mel nodded. Alvin shook his head and cursed. As the two prospectors ducked through the corral fence, heading for the livery barn's rear doors, Longarm hefted the Henry and began hoofing it back the way he'd come, keeping a keen eye out for Little-Boy's men.

He'd covered about half the length of the alley when the muffled clomp of hooves and the rattle of heavy wagons rose from the main street to his right. Men whooped and yelled, and horses whinnied above the thunder of the wagons.

Freighters, no doubt. Judging by the din sluicing down the gaps between buildings, they were entering Happiness from the east.

Even moving cautiously, it didn't take Longarm ten minutes to reach the rear of the jailhouse. No smoke ribboned from the chimney pipe. Not surprising that no one had bothered to stoke the stove for Mojave Joe.

The lawman snugged his shoulder against the back side of the stone building, pausing to inspect his back trail. Seeing no one, he slipped around the jailhouse's east rear corner and tramped along the wall, holding the cocked Henry up high across his chest. At the front corner, he dropped to a knee and edged a look into the street.

There were several horses lined up in front of Miss

Sylvania's House of Ill Repute, and someone was hammering away at the piano inside while smoke buffeted above the twin rock chimneys.

Most of the commotion was occurring in the street before the general store. Three freight wagons were pulled up to the loading dock, and a half dozen burly men in heavy fur coats or mackinaws were off-loading crates, barrels, and burlap sacks.

The tall, gaunt proprietor stood at the edge of the dock, a long bear coat draping his shoulders. He held a clipboard in one hand, a pencil in the other, as he watched the unloading carefully, checking off items on his list. A beefy, red-haired gent stood to his right, talking, laughing, and smoking a thick cigar.

Behind them, the hairy, wizened old man called Ebeneezer stood holding a steaming coffee mug, chatting about the weather with one of the off-loading freighters. When the freighter turned in the direction of the jailhouse, flinging an arm out to point along his back trail, Longarm pulled his head back behind the corner of the jailhouse.

He winced, squeezing the Henry rifle in both gloved hands.

Had he been spotted?

The freighter and Ebeneezer continued chatting, and the crates and barrels continued thumping and barking onto the loading dock.

Longarm waited there at the corner of the jailhouse, one knee in the snow, listening and keeping an eye on the street and gauging the time mentally, as his railroad-grade Ingersoll had been lost to the frigid creek. He needed to get into Miss Sylvania's place well ahead of the prospectors blowing the barn, but he wanted to see what had become of Mojave Joe, though he had a pretty good idea.

Chief Marshal Billy Vail wasn't going to like it. Letting a prisoner freeze to death didn't exactly jibe with the lawmen's code of ethics.

After what seemed an hour but probably had been only seven or eight minutes, all the freight had been back-and-bellied onto the loading dock. Edging a look around the jailhouse corner, Longarm watched the proprietor and the beefy, red-haired gent—the freight crew's ramrod, no doubt—retreat into the general store, the beefy gent laughing overloud and clapping the proprietor's back.

The five other freighters, grunting and jeering each other good-naturedly, obviously relieved the chill trip up the mountain was over, started hefting the freight from the dock and into the store itself. When all had disappeared inside at the same time, Longarm bounded around the corner of the jailhouse, tripped the door latch, and slipped inside.

Quietly latching the door behind him, he peered into the shadows at the rear of the room. His heart skipped a beat.

The door of the cell in which he'd locked Mojave Joe stood wide open.

Chapter 16

Looking around the jailhouse warily, as though expecting the outlaw to bolt out from hiding, a six-gun blazing, Longarm moved slowly toward the open cell, holding the Henry's butt against his hip, the barrel aimed at the cell's dense shadows trimmed in gray.

Just outside the cell, he stopped, raked his gaze across the single cot with rumpled blankets, the tin plate and rusty spoon on the floor beneath, the slop bucket in the far corner, its lid resting upside down beside it.

No Joe.

Longarm had expected to find the outlaw curled up, hard as granite, on his cot. Someone had let the bastard out.

Voices rose outside. Longarm jerked around with a start, tensing his trigger finger as he aimed the Henry at the jailhouse's closed front door, heart thumping.

It was only the freighters joking around over at the general store.

He raised the rifle, moved to the window on the door's left side, and peered out. Three of the freighters were tramping across the street toward Miss Sylvania's House of Ill Repute. Two were mock-fighting and trading insults while the third followed close on their heels, lifting his chin to whoop, "I done been savin' my pennies, so I'm headin' all the way up to the *third floor!*"

Meanwhile, the other two freighters were swinging the empty wagons around to head back in the direction from which they'd come—no doubt intending to stable the mules and the wagons before heading over to the whorehouse themselves.

Longarm looked around the office once more, glancing at the open cell door. Where was Mojave Joe? Had one of Little-Boy's men let him out, or had he convinced someone else to spring him?

Although the thought of Mojave Joe running amok around Happiness lifted the hair on the back of his neck, Longarm didn't have time to worry about the outlaw at the moment. He had bigger fish to fry.

He looked across the street. The freighters were mounting the porch fronting the whorehouse, still jeering and roughhousing while the chickadees and nuthatches milled about the feeder. The wagons had pulled on past the jailhouse, making for the livery barn sitting kitty-corner across the street.

Longarm turned back to the whorehouse. The freighters stood grouped on the porch, facing each other, digging around in their pockets and holding out coins and greenbacks, as though figuring how much time upstairs and at the poker tables they could afford. One man turned to the one who'd been saving his pennies, apparently beseeching the flush gent for a loan.

Longarm turned from the window and reached for the doorknob. He stopped, glanced down at the rifle. He'd had no problem entering the whorehouse with his six-shooter, but he doubted Miss Sylvania would let him get past the front door with the Henry. Even if she would let him, the rifle would draw too much attention.

He set the rifle against the door casing, opened the door, and looked out. The three freighters still arguing on the whorehouse porch were the only men about, and none was looking toward the jailhouse.

Closing the door behind him, Longarm lowered Mel's patch down over his eye and tramped into the street. He pulled the three-point capote's collar up around his neck, the coonskin cap down low over his brows, and shuffled toward the whorehouse, dragging his left leg as though he'd destroyed the knee, as miners were prone to do, in his ever-zealous quest for gold.

The limp might be going too far, but it couldn't hurt.

He began limping up the steps, using the railing and breathing hard and grinning drunkenly—hooch being another miner's weakness, especially in winter—and gained the top just as the freighters were filing into the whorehouse. Off-key piano notes and boisterous laughter wafted through the open door on a wave of warm air thick with the smell of liquor, perfume, and cheap tobacco.

Longarm figured that by entering Miss Sylvania's on the heels of the freighters, he'd be given less scrutiny and the opportunity to disappear more quickly into the crowd. He was right. The derbie-wearing, bung starter–wielding thug at the bottom of the entryway's three steps glanced at each freighter in turn, using the same turn of his head to quickly scrutinize Longarm. Scowling with barely concealed disgust, he waved the men, including Longarm, on inside Miss Sylvania's main drinking and gambling hall, the carpet somewhat muffling the din rising from the crowd of a good thirty or forty drinking, gambling, smoking, whore-sparking men.

A dapper little man in a checked suit with a fox shawl was hammering away at the piano, a beer and a shot glass within easy reach and a cornhusk cigarette tucked in the corner of his mouth. Dragging his left leg and wincing with the effort, Longarm followed the freighters to the bar on the left side of the room.

Keeping his chin down and his cap pulled low over his eyes, he squeezed between two other men in business suits and sidled up to the mahogany, trying not to make eye contact with the bartender—the same man who'd tended him on his first visit to the whorehouse. He rested his left elbow on the bar as he shuttled his gaze across the smoky room, trying hard to look casual. His gut tightened when he saw the stocky, rusty-haired gent, Cody, strolling around the gambling tables twirling a bung starter. His beady eyes appeared especially close to the nose Longarm had broken, swollen up to the size of a door stop. The thick, white bandage stood out from the room's smoky shadows like a white flag of surrender on a crowded battlefield—though Longarm doubted there would be any surrender from Cody if he spied Longarm under the coonskin cap and behind the eye patch.

The lawman's gut drew even tauter when he spied Little-Boy standing on the far side of the room, legs spread, arms crossed on his broad chest. The big, long-haired, flat-faced Indian puffed a fat cigar as he scrutinized the half dozen men at the clacking and clattering roulette wheel on the far side of the broad, carpeted stairs. An ivory-gripped Remington jutted butt-forward on Little-Boy's left hip while a large knife and a bung starter were strapped to the right.

While Longarm stared at the man, remembering Mel's account of the beating that had resulted in his empty eye socket, a drunk prospector with a bib beard ran into Little-Boy. It was like running into a parked, loaded freight wagon. Little-Boy didn't so much as sway. He glared down at the man, whose nearly bald head was level with Little-Boy's biceps, bunching his thick lips and muttering something Longarm couldn't hear above the ceaseless din. The bib-bearded gent held up his hands in supplication, bowing and truckling, as he backed away toward one of the poker tables.

Longarm ground his molars as he imagined burying Mel's bowie in the big man's gut. Then he glanced at the stairs. Somehow, he had to get to the third floor. He'd like to have a good head start by the time Mel and Alvin blew the livery barn.

He was deep in agitated thought when someone tapped his shoulder. He swung his head around with a start. The scar-faced bartender with the cobalt eyes was scowling at him from across the bar. "I said, what'll it be, bub? If you ain't gonna order a drink, *vamoose*!"

Longarm hesitated, heart hammering as he avoided the man's stare. If the barkeep recognized him behind the eye patch, his goose was not only cooked but served up piping hot with potatoes and gravy.

"Beer!" Longarm yelled above the din, quickly turning back toward the room.

When the barman set the beer in front of Longarm's elbow, the lawman tossed him a dime, which he caught out of the air and dropped into his apron pocket before moving on to the next customer. Longarm let out a slow sigh as he lifted the frothy mug of musky, molasses-dark beer to his lips and glanced across the room once more as he sipped.

Sylvania Thayer was a little harder to pick out of the

crowd than Little-Boy and Cody. Just as Longarm's eyes found her, sitting in the near-middle of the room with a half dozen gamblers and the blond dove, Casey, who sat in the lap of one of the men, nibbling his earlobe, the wheelchair-bound madam turned suddenly toward Little-Boy. She pointed to one of the men at the table, who rose, rubbing his hands together eagerly. Little-Boy nodded curtly and, removing his cigar from his mouth, began slouching toward the stairs.

As the gambler plopped several greenbacks down in front of Sylvania Thayer and turned toward the stairs, Longarm's heart picked up. If he could buy some time with one of the Chinese girls, he'd be upstairs in no time. But first he'd have to pay Miss Sylvania, who'd no doubt recognize him. And, if she didn't, Little-Boy, who apparently did all the escorting of the men to the third story, certainly would.

Maybe he could at least get to the second story before Little-Boy closed that trapdoor staircase.

At the rear of the room, Little-Boy leaned behind the piano, which the dapper gent continued to pound maniacally, then turned back toward the room. He held a long, wooden pole with a hook at the end. Holding the pole negligently over his shoulder, he gave the gambler a stony glance, then started up the stairs.

The gambler paused at the bottom of the stairs to adjust his crisp bowler, giving the hat a rakish tilt over one eye, then started up the stairs about five steps behind Little-Boy.

"I heard them Chinese were a prime fuck!" Longarm could hear him shout drunkenly, raising his spade-bearded chin toward the Indian.

Little-Boy hiked a shoulder as he topped the stairs. Longarm watched until both men disappeared into the second story, then glanced at the clock behind the bar. He probably had about five minutes before Mel and Alvin blew the livery barn. He had to get upstairs before the barn blew or, especially if Sylvania or Little-Boy savvied the ploy, he might not have enough time to get the girls out.

Pretending a leisurely sip from his beer mug, he pushed away from the bar in his haste to find a way upstairs, nearly forgetting to drag his left leg. He traced a circuitous route between tables, dragging the leg and avoiding the rusty-headed Cody and Sylvania Thayer.

Could he get up the steps without being seen by Sylvania or one of the thugs?

The thought had just crossed his mind when, dragging his leg around a group of standing, bearded men conversing in thick German accents, someone stepped out of nowhere to trip over his left foot. The man stumbled back behind Longarm and almost dropped to a knee before getting both feet beneath him.

"Hey, watch where the hell you're goin', gimp!"

The familiar voice sent a razor-edged icicle through Longarm's heart.

He half turned toward the man, in an instant taking in the tall, gangly frame and pewter mustache and hair and the flat, pinched-together eyes of Mojave Joe. The outlaw wore a cheap suit and vest and a bowler hat tipped low over his shaggy pewter brows. In his right hand he squeezed a bung starter so tight that his knuckles were white as bone. A snarl curled his upper lip, and his cheeks were red with rage.

The bastard had moved up in the world.

Longarm jerked his head forward and threw a hand out in apology as he continued shuffling toward the stairs, his ears ringing, expecting that bung starter to arc toward him at any second.

"And just where in the hell do you think you're goin'?" Joe barked behind him.

Chapter 17

In the corner of his left eye, Longarm saw Mojave Joe lumbering toward him.

He prepared to lose the limp and reach inside his coat for his Colt but stopped the motion when another figure materialized to fall into step beside him and wrap her left arm around Longarm's right.

"He's headin' upstairs with me, Joe," said Dominique, the beautiful, full-busted, redheaded whore. She gripped his arm tightly and leaned toward him as they started up the stairs together. She gritted her teeth and kept her voice just beneath a whisper. "What in the hell are you doing *back* here, idiot?"

"Why, Miss Dominique," Longarm said, gritting his own teeth edgily, feeling Mojave Joe's eyes boring into his back and still half expecting the bung starter to lay his head open. "What an unexpected surprise."

"I thought for sure they'd killed you," she said, rubbing her left breast against his arm as he limped along beside her, glancing out the corner of his eye at Mojave Joe still standing at the bottom of the stairs. "I heard Little-Boy getting his firebrands together to douse your fire."

"They came right close. Luckily, my fire burns hot."

Dominique shot a quick glance over her shoulder. "Keep limping, and pray Miss Sylvania doesn't notice. She always demands to be paid in person before we take a man to our room."

"Trusting soul, ain't she?" Longarm quipped, trying to ease the tension, which felt like a ramrod shoved up his spine.

It took the patience of Job for Longarm to maintain the limp while presenting his broad back to the saloon hall full of thugs, including Mojave Joe staring up at him menacingly. When he and Dominique gained the top of the stairs and turned down the hall, he loosed a long sigh of relief, abandoning the limp and taking long strides toward the trapdoor stairs hanging from the ceiling like a drooping dragon's tongue.

Deep voices tumbled through the opening, including that of Little-Boy. Springs squawked, and there was the tap-tap-tap of a bed frame hitting a wall.

Longarm paused to stare up through the dark opening, glimpsing flickering candlelight and lantern light and the shadows of moving figures. He began moving toward the bottom of the steps.

Dominique grabbed his arm and jerked him toward the door of her room. "What—are you *crazy*? Little-Boy's up there!"

Longarm resisted the girl's tug on his arm for only a second. While the open stairs were enticing as hell, going up there now before the men downstairs were distracted would be sure suicide.

He'd gained the second story. He'd have to wait now until the prospectors blew the barn—which they should have done by now, as their hour was up—before attempting the third.

He stumbled into Dominique's room. She peered out fearfully, casting her gaze up through the trapdoor, then quickly closed the door and turned to Longarm. "You're crazy, aren't you? You've got to be crazy."

"I've been dropped on my head a few times," Longarm said, shoving Mel's eye patch onto his forehead and glancing at the marble-cased clock over the girl's dresser. "But if all goes well, I should have those Chinese girls out within fifteen minutes or so."

Dominique moved to him, set her hands on his chest, and pushed him back toward the bed. "Pull your pants down."

"Huh?"

"Little-Boy's been checking on me. He's suspicious. Now, pull your pants down. We've got to look convincing in case he pokes his head in the door when he comes back down from upstairs."

"I don't have time for—"

Kneeling between his own knees, she glared up at him. "Pull 'em down or I'll scream for Little-Boy!"

Longarm cursed and unbuckled his cartridge belt. He set the gun and holster beside him, then pulled his trousers and underwear bottoms down to his knees. He felt silly and exposed, but if it was the only way to skin the cat . . .

He cursed again when the girl leaned toward him and grabbed his limp dong, chagrined to feel, despite the dire circumstances, a dull twinge of lust in his cock, which began to slowly roust itself like a sleeping snake sensing prey.

The girl stared up at him, keeping her hand wrapped around his dong for appearances. "How in the hell do you intend to pull this off?"

"You'll see." Longarm was leaning back on his elbows, waiting for the explosion while listening for Little-Boy, anxiety racking him, wondering what the hell could have happened to Alvin and Mel. "Once I'm upstairs, will you help me get the girls down?"

"If you'll take me with you."

Longarm stared at her.

"I can't take this life anymore," she said. "If you can call it a life—imprisoned here, having to fuck every unwashed rock picker within thirty square miles for only food and a place to sleep. When they *let* me sleep." She raised her dark glance to the ceiling. "After what happened to Madeleine, I'm ready to end it all, like another one of the Chinese girls did only last week."

"What happened to Madeleine?"

Dominique lowered her incredulous gaze to Longarm's crotch. "Jesus Christ!"

He looked down. He wasn't fully aroused, but close, his member growing steadily, the girl's small, pale hand wrapped around the base. "Ignore it. What happened to Madeleine?"

"Miss Sylvania had Little-Boy kill her." Dominique opened her mouth to continue but stopped when foot thuds sounded on the stairs, growing louder. Quickly, the girl lowered her head to Longarm's crotch, dropped her mouth over the head.

He groaned, sucked a sharp breath.

As the commotion continued into the hall, men laughing and arguing, boots thumping, Dominique continued to suck and speak by turns, bobbing her head.

"Miss Sylvania found out Madeleine and the Happiness lawmen . . . were going to raid the place and spring the Chinese . . . well, Sylvania got to the lawmen first . . . and to Madeleine . . ."

"I found the constable and Madeleine," Longarm said tightly as Dominique sank her lips down over his cock once more. "What about the deputies?"

She pulled her head back up and over his swollen head, spittle stringing from her lips, and gazed up at him sharply. "They're the ones you found hanging from the dead tree on Newton's Bench. Little-Boy did it, left 'em to hang as a warning to any other lawmen in the area who might get the same idea about triflin' with his and his ma's business."

Dominique lowered her head, her wet lips making crackling sounds as she continued to work, warily rolling her eyes toward the door.

Longarm's loins burned with lust, and he groaned. He didn't know if it was the dicey situation or merely the girl's abilities, but he hadn't had a blow job this raw and delightful in a long time, and he found himself hoping she could finish before Mel and Alvin blew the barn.

He ground his fingers into the bed, and hesitated before asking, "One of the deputies was in love with Madeleine, I take it?"

Dominique nodded, gave an especially thrilling suck before lifting her head. "Along with half the town. Madeleine was a professional . . . it half-killed Miss Sylvania to kill her . . . but not because of any love lost between them . . . she'd become a threat to her bus—"

Dominique stopped and, holding Longarm's wet, piston-stiff cock in both hands, turned sharply toward the door. Boots thudded on the trapdoor stairs—heavy boots moving slowly and deliberately, a big man breathing heavily. There was a clattering thud and twang of springs as the stairs were shoved back into the ceiling. The man swiped his hands together. The floor creaked beneath his boots, and a shadow showed through the crack under the door.

The doorknob turned slowly.

Dominique gasped and turned back to Longarm, who

quickly lowered Mel's patch over his eye. The girl dropped her head once more over his shaft. Longarm's heart thudded as the latch clicked and the door opened, the crack between the frame and the door filling with the big, dark face and hatchet nose of Little-Boy.

Longarm resisted the urge to grab his .44 and start shooting. He threw his head back on his shoulders and groaned as the girl continued plying her trade between his knees—up and down, up and down, her hot tongue artfully flicking and caressing even in her terror of the big man peering through the open door behind her.

Longarm's blood boiled in his churning loins.

Peeking through his closed lids at Little-Boy peering back at him through the quarter-open door, he ground his fingers into the feather-stuffed mattress, heart rolling and heaving from a combination of fear, fury, and nearly unbearable erotic bliss.

Little-Boy scowled, long hair framing his face, broad nostrils flaring.

The girl's exquisite head, with its lush, red hair pinned high, pistoned up and down frantically.

Staring back at Little-Boy from beneath his closed lids, Longarm began edging his right hand toward the walnut grips of his Colt. He held off when the big Indian turned his mouth corners down. Little-Boy gave a satisfied snort, drew his head back through the opening, and pulled the door closed behind him.

When the latch clicked, Dominique lifted her head and started to turn toward the door with a sigh.

"Hold on!" Longarm rasped, flailing at her with his hands and drawing her back down on his shaft.

She gave a start and, gagging slightly, dropped her head down to his crotch. He ground his hands once more into the mattress as his cock slid down the girl's expanding and contracting throat.

Throwing his head back and hardening his jaws, he loosed a shrill groan as his loins exploded like a mail car rigged with nitroglycerin. The girl rose up on his knees but kept her head low, gagging and groaning as his seed jettisoned down her throat, the head of his cock snugged deep between her tonsils.

Still gagging and choking, Dominique was just beginning to slide her lips back toward the end of Longarm's cock when what sounded like mountain thunder nearby rocked the building, making the lanterns and windowpanes sing. The girl's eyes widened as, placing a hand to her chest and swallowing hard, she gaped up at Longarm.

"Jesus, when you shoot your load, you really *shoot your load!*"

Longarm had jerked his head up at the sound. Mel and Alvin had finally blown the barn—though, judging by the size of the explosion, they'd taken more than the barn. Catching her breath, recovering from her French lesson, Dominique opened her mouth to speak once more, but Longarm held up a hand, shushing her.

Downstairs, the piano had fallen silent, but the din continued with an exclamatory, incredulous edge, Sylvania Thayer herself yelling above the raucous roar of inquiring voices, "*What* the *hell* was *that?*"

The din rose even louder, and there was another, softer roar as the crowd downstairs began marching across the carpeted saloon hall toward the doors and windows. Sylvania Thayer yelled for Little-Boy and then started barking orders, or what sounded to Longarm like orders—he could no longer hear clearly above the crowd's collective, incredulous clamoring.

163

Above Longarm's head, the rafters rocked and squawked as men stomped into boots. "Nils, pull your dick out!" a man barked in the third story. "Somethin's burning on the other end of town. I can see it through the shutter!"

"Fire?" Nils returned, the voice owning to the camp dweller's mind-numbing fear of a conflagration. *"Fuck!"*

Men yelled and bustled about on all three stories. Hall doors opened and closed. Curses rose. One of the whores bellowed, "That's my bottle, you bastard!"

Longarm reached down for his pants.

"What the hell's goin' on?" Dominique said, still on her knees and staring incredulously up at the lawman.

"We're about to get the Chinese girls out of that third-story cave." Longarm stood and pulled his pants up around his waist. "Get yourself into some warm duds, pronto. Do the Chinese have coats and hats and such?"

"I doubt it," Dominique said, frowning as she rose from her knees, still trying to understand what was happening. "What would they need them for? They're not allowed outside."

Longarm was strapping on his shell belt when the trapdoor opened suddenly with a raucous bark and a loud thud as it hit the hall floor.

"Goddamnit!" a man bellowed as his boots pounded the creaky steps. "My store's right across the street from that barn!"

"Well, shit, you know where my barbershop's at. I lose that, I lose *everything*!"

As both men charged past Dominique's door and down the hall toward the stairs, Longarm snugged his coonskin cap down low on his forehead once more and moved to the door.

"Fire!" Sylvania Thayer was bellowing, sounding more

bobcat than human. "Fire at the other end of town! Fire, ye hear, boys? *Fi-rrrrrre!*"

Longarm twisted the knob, cracked the door, and peeked out. The doors to his left were all open, a couple of the working girls standing in the doorways in various stages of undress, peering out warily. To Longarm's right, another door opened, and a scrawny, balding gent with wire-rimmed spectacles dashed out of a room, clutching his clothes against his chest. He sprinted off toward the stairs, and the sound of his bare feet on the carpeted steps was drowned by the dwindling din.

It sounded as though most of the men, following Sylvania Thayer's orders, had headed outside to contain the fire while Sylvania Thayer herself continued bellowing, *"Fire! Put out that goddamn fire!"*

Longarm glanced at Dominique, who stood wringing her hands and staring at him from the middle of the room.

"Damnit, girl, get dressed!"

With that, he drew the door wide, dashed into the hall, and headed up the stairs. Behind him, someone laughed heartily. It was half a whoop and half a rebel yell.

Longarm stopped three steps up from the hall floor.

The laugh had a chillingly familiar ring to it.

"Longarm, you old dog—where the hell you think you're goin', anyways?"

Longarm's chest fell with a plaintively expelled breath. Scowling, he turned to look over his shoulder.

Mojave Joe stood about fifteen feet from the bottom of the trapdoor stairs, moving toward Longarm, grinning, holding a cocked Sharps rifle straight out from his hip.

Chapter 18

Longarm heard a couple of the whores standing in their open doorways up and down the hall give startled grunts and groans as they watched Mojave Joe bear down on him, aiming the Sharps buffalo gun at Longarm's belly.

Mojave Joe chuckled. "That's a damn good getup. You almost had me fooled. Soon as you made the top of the stairs, I realized it was you." The outlaw slitted one eye as he stopped about ten feet from Longarm, raising the Sharps to his shoulder. "What the hell's so damn enticin' up there, anyway? They got gold stashed?"

Holding his hands chest high, Longarm turned on the steps, awkwardly keeping his balance. His thoughts raced. He had to buy some time. But at the *same* time, Little-Boy and Miss Sylvania, who were still bellowing downstairs like lynxes caught in spring traps, would soon figure out that the explosion had been a diversion.

Little-Boy and the entire male population of Happiness would bound up the stairs with their hoglegs drawn.

"Never mind," Joe said, squinting down the Sharps's barrel. "I'll find out for mys—"

A pistol popped. Joe's head jerked sideways. The outlaw

took one step in the same direction, wobbling on his boots and dropping the buffalo gun with a dull thud.

He sidled up against the wall, knocking a candle sconce askew. Standing there for several seconds, he stared at Longarm with a puzzled expression. He blinked as though to clear his eyes, slowly canting his head as though it were too heavy to hold straight on his shoulders. Blood began welling from his left ear, dribbling down over the lobe to his neck.

Joe gave a clipped groan and dropped to his knees. He fell forward, hitting the floor on his face, legs twitching as the life left him.

"Who in the hell's shootin' up there?" Miss Sylvania bellowed from the bottom of the stairs as Longarm turned toward the open door of Dominique's room. "And why in the hell ain't you outside fightin' the *fire*?"

Dominique stood in her room's doorway, staring down at Mojave Joe. A gold-plated derringer sagged in her right hand, smoke curling from the barrel. She wore a man's oversized quilted canvas coat, a fur hat, baggy blue denims, and fur-trimmed moccasins.

"Christ," the girl rasped. "Is he dead?"

Longarm nodded and muttered, "There ya go, Buster. That one's for you." He glanced around the hall as several doors closed, the other doves sensing trouble and wanting no part of it. Ignoring Sylvania Thayer's bellowed demands from the bottom of the stairs, he looked at Dominique and canted his head toward the hole above. "Come on."

He swung around and climbed the last four steps, rising through the hole into the smoky third story rife with the smell of raw liquor, sweat, sex, and opium. Moving away from the hole, he glanced around at the bare, papered walls and the wool blankets and quilts hanging from ropes. Behind the blankets were crude plank beds, spittoons, crude wash-stands, and dressers, one of which boasted a cracked mirror.

It was a coarse living area, little better than a large jail cell. The customers no doubt didn't mind. In fact, the crude conditions probably enhanced the atmosphere of forbidden pleasure.

Two girls with round faces and slanted, dark eyes sat on a bed on each side of the aisle, both sitting with their backs to the outside wall, legs drawn up to their chests. One wore a black robe embroidered with small goldfish, her thick, black hair piled high atop her regal head. The flat planes of her young face were smeared with rouge. Her slender legs were bare, her toes painted bright red. On a small table beside her, a porcelain opium pipe burned.

The other girl wore nothing except pantaloons and slippers. No more than twelve or thirteen, she'd crossed her arms on her nubbin breasts. As Longarm approached, she sidled up to the wall, as though trying to merge with it. Her long, straight, disheveled hair framed her face, which was also gaudied up with rouge.

Both girls regarded Longarm as though he were a rogue grizzly sure to kill and devour them. The youngest sobbed, her pale, fragile shoulders jerking, tears further smearing the face paint.

"It's all right," Longarm said, raising his hands benignly. "I'm not gonna hurt you. I'm gonna get you out of here."

As he passed between the two girls, he heard more sob-bing and groaning in the smoky shadows beyond. Ahead, a blanket was drawn across the aisle. The sobs seemed to rise from behind it. Longarm approached slowly, one arm on his .44's grips.

From outside rose the muffled shouts and exclamations

of the men fighting the fire. Sylvania Thayer had fallen eerily silent.

Longarm pulled the blanket aside suddenly. He froze, his revolver half out of its holster. Before him, on a broad, plank bed covered with twisted quilts, another Chinese girl lay. This one was slightly taller and more filled out than the others, but she was still probably under twenty. Her hair was cut off short. She lay flat on her back, naked, wrists and ankles tied to each of the bed's four posts. A red and white neckerchief had been tied around her face, gagging her.

She'd jerked with a start when she'd first seen Longarm. Now, she stared in terror up at him, her breasts rising and falling sharply as she breathed. Tears dribbled down her cheeks to her neck. Her lower lip was swollen and scabbed. Her pale breasts and legs were chafed.

"Christ!" Longarm rasped, dropping the Colt back into its holster.

He reached down and removed Mel's bowie knife from his ankle scabbard. Spying the knife, the girl's eyes widened and flashed in horror. She squirmed around, pulling at the rawhide ties and groaning around the gag as Longarm moved to the cot and quickly hacked through each ankle tie in turn.

"It's all right, honey—I ain't gonna hurt you."

He reached behind her neck to remove the gag, then hacked through the rawhide rope tying her wrists to the bed's front posts. The girl stared up at him, eyes no longer terrified as much as wary and puzzled. She uttered something in an incomprehensible tongue as she lifted her head and massaged her left wrist.

"I don't know what you're sayin'. You understand any English at all?"

The girl pulled her legs in and continued staring up at

him, the skin above the bridge of her nose wrinkling as she shook her head slightly.

Longarm cursed under his breath. He whipped around and pushed back out into the main room. Dominique was near the cot of the youngest Chinese girl, bending down to peer at the floor beneath.

"Get 'em dressed," Longarm told her. "I'm gonna go down and see how we're doin'."

"This is insane," Dominique said, lifting her head above the top of the youngest girl's cot and casting a plaintive gaze at Longarm. "All they have is underclothes and robes!"

Longarm tramped back toward the trapdoor, holding his .44 down low in his right hand. "Put as many duds on 'em as you can, and wrap 'em in blankets and quilts. If you have to, tie pillowcases around their feet. Then get 'em downstairs as fast as you can."

He stopped near the rectangular hole filled with wan gray light and turned back to Dominique. "But it ain't too late to change your mind. I'd understand."

Dominique stared back at him for a stretched moment, then heaved a sigh. She began scurrying around, gathering underclothes. "If I'm gonna die, I'd rather die on my feet. Come on, Kim-Su," she said, tossing the other Chinese girl a quilt. "We're getting the hell out of here!"

Longarm dropped down the steps, raising his revolver as he gained the second-floor hall. Mojave Joe lay where Dominique had drilled him, blood puddling the carpet runner beneath his right ear. All of the hall doors except Dominique's were closed, and the entire building had fallen silent, though outside dogs were barking and men were yelling. There was the clatter of wooden buckets.

The men had no doubt formed a bucket brigade from the creek, trying to put the fire out before it involved the

171

whole town. In spite of the recent snow, the log and wood-frame buildings were likely dry as well-seasoned tinder.

Longarm hurried down the hall and turned the corner at the top of the stairs. As he started down, his heart leapt. Sylvania Thayer sat her wheelchair at the bottom, aiming a double-bore shotgun up the steps, the stock pressed against her cheek. Longarm threw himself back around the hall corner as the right bore spat smoke and flames.

KA-BOOM!

The thundering blast in the close quarters felt like a cupped palm slapped against his ears. He hit the hall floor on his right shoulder as the old woman bellowed, "Tryin' to fetch away my Chinese pussy, are ye? Well, lawdog, you got another *think comin'*!"

KA-BOOM!

The second blast of buckshot peppered the wall at the top of the stairs and chewed wood from the corner in front of Longarm.

"No one steals my Chink pussy!" the old woman bellowed.

Longarm scrambled back to his feet and, holding his cocked Colt straight out before him, hurried around the hall corner and dropped down the stairs two steps at a time, the old, pinch-faced woman growing before him, her smoking shotgun angled across her blanket-draped lap.

"Hold it there, you fuckin' bitch!" Longarm ordered, running his left hand along the scrolled rail, his boots thudding on the carpeted steps.

Sylvania Thayer squinted her eyes and lifted her chin, cackling. "Wouldn't shoot a crippled old woman, would ya?"

Longarm was two-thirds of the way down the steps when she hauled up a pearl-gripped, double-barreled derringer from beneath the blanket.

"Stop!" Longarm shouted.

The old woman grinned as she cocked and raised the derringer, extending it straight out from her shoulder, squinting down the barrel.

Longarm stopped, aimed quickly, and drilled the crippled madam through her right shoulder. She screamed. Clutching her wounded shoulder with one hand, she triggered the derringer into the stair rail's newel post with the other.

"Little-Boy!" she wailed, throwing her head back on her shoulders. *"Little-Boyyyy!"*

She cocked the derringer once more, angled it up toward Longarm.

He shot her again, his second slug drilling a quarter-sized hole through the middle of her pale, wrinkled forehead. Her head snapped straight back against the chair back, and the chair itself squawked backward into the saloon hall. The shotgun dropped from the dying madam's lap to hit the floor with a heavy, clattering thud. The derringer followed a second later, tumbling from her gnarled, slackening fingers.

"Jesus H. Christ! You sure cleaned Miss Sylvania's old clock!" It was Alvin, standing left of the stairs, holding his Spencer rifle and facing the dead madam, whose chair had hung up on the carpet about halfway between the stairs and the front door.

Longarm continued down the steps, hearing voices growing louder outside, as though several of the men, having heard the gunfire, were racing back toward the saloon. "Alvin, what the hell took you so long?"

The old graybeard glanced at Longarm. The shoulders of his ragged coat were trimmed with large, downy snowflakes. "Them old fuses went bad. We had to break into Ralph Peck's place for his." He chuckled. "Ralph's worked just fine, as you mighta heard. We got the mules out back, even picked up a couple saddle hosses along the way!"

Replacing the spent shells in his Colt's cylinder, Longarm jogged toward Miss Sylvania, sagging in her wheelchair, eyes open and glaring. He canted his head toward the ceiling. "Get upstairs and help Dominique with the Chinese girls. I'll cover the front!"

Mumbling and grunting, Alvin started up the stairs. Longarm continued toward the front of the room. There were a half dozen rifles lined up to the right of the door. Customers' rifles. Longarm grabbed a Winchester carbine, made sure it was loaded, racked a fresh shell into the chamber, then tramped over to the window to the left of the door.

Four men were running toward the saloon, within forty yards and closing. Behind them, heavy, gray black smoke billowed, screening off the other half of the town. Flames broiled above the smoke, through which Longarm caught glimpses of men scurrying around with wooden water buckets, yelling and cursing and barking orders. It was hard to tell, but judging by the smoke and flames, the fire had spread to three or four buildings and was threatening more.

Longarm waited till the four men—two of whom were the broken-nosed thug, Cody, and the bartender—were about ten feet from the porch. Then he stepped outside quickly and rested the Winchester's barrel across his shoulder.

Chapter 19

Cody spied Longarm first, his head snapping up. He stopped abruptly, throwing one arm out in front of the bartender. "Look!"

The other three men stopped and looked up at the porch. They all wore heavy coats, hats, and gloves. Three wielded pistols. Only one carried a Winchester; he held it in both hands across his chest. The bartender's cobalt eyes seized on Longarm like the twin bores of a particularly deadly gun. He grinned, but there wasn't any humor in it.

"What the fuck's your game, mister?"

"Deputy United States marshal," Longarm said. "And you boys are headin' in the wrong direction. Miss Sylvania's House of Ill Repute has done been closed down."

The four were spread out in the street and off to the left of the porch steps. Longarm had a clear view over the porch rail. In spite of the fire and the billowing smoke, the winter birds continued to wheel and caterwaul around the feeder, half the seeds of which littered the porch to his right.

Behind the men facing him, the others shouted above the loudening roar of the fire.

Longarm cast a quick, wary glance from left to right, raking his gaze across the buildings fronting the street.

Where was Little-Boy?

He brought his glance back to the four men glaring up at him. The man with the Winchester was opening and closing his gloved hands around it, narrowing his eyes nervously.

"Shit, friend," Cody said, his voice sounding nasal through his broken nose, "that's done been tried before, you big, stupid son of a bitch."

Longarm stared calmly down over the porch steps and canted his head to one side. He hoped Alvin and Dominique were getting the Chinese girls downstairs and outside. He couldn't hold off the entire town.

"I don't think there's any call for name-callin'," he said.

The four just stared up at him, cautious, wary. Cody squinted one eye and canted his head toward the bartender. "You think he's alone?"

"He's stupid. But he ain't *that* stupid."

"No," one of the others said. Longarm recognized both him and the fourth man from the hill above the stream— the men who had nearly killed him. "He's got someone inside tryin' to squirrel them Chinese out the back. I'd bet a nut on it."

Longarm wasn't sure if the bartender or Cody began whipping his revolver up first. They both moved at nearly the same time. Having sensed it coming, Longarm had begun edging the Winchester off his shoulder.

He slapped the forestock into the palm of his left gloved hand and squeezed the trigger, blowing Cody straight up and back. Before Cody hit the ground, the bartender was tumbling back beside him, blood and brains spewing from his left temple.

Longarm's Winchester continued roaring, and only one

of the other two thugs was able to snap off an errant shot before both men were sent twisting around and rolling as they yelled and screamed behind the wafting cloud of powder smoke.

Longarm's empty shell casings clinked onto the porch floor behind him.

Catching movement out the corner of his right eye, Longarm whipped his head around as a bullet clipped his earlobe and plunked into the whorehouse's front door. The rifle's bark reached him a quarter-second later.

Little-Boy bolted out of the gap between two log buildings on the other side of the street. The big man held a rifle in one hand, a revolver in the other, and his long buffalo robe flapped about his long, bowed legs as he sprinted toward Longarm, triggering each weapon in turn.

Bullets buzzed around Longarm's head and plunked into the wall behind him.

Knowing he had no time to rack a fresh shell and aim, he twisted left and bounded off his right foot, propelling himself toward the large, plate-glass window to the right of the whorehouse's front door.

His forearms and the Winchester hit the glass with a scream of shattering panes. As the rest of his body followed, glass rained around him. He heard at least two more lead bumblebees buzzing through the hail of glass to plunk into an awning post and a coat rack just inside the whorehouse's main hall.

He hit the floor on his left shoulder and rolled onto his back as another slug careened through the air a foot above his head to plunk into an oil painting of a naked, big-breasted blonde riding a high-stepping white stallion through a lush, green forest.

"Jumpin' Jehoshaphat!"

Longarm glanced left. The graybearded Alvin was making his way down the broad stairs at the rear of the room, the three Chinese girls following while clutching quilts or blankets about their shoulders. Dominique brought up the rear in her man's duds, long red hair falling from her fur hat to sweep across the shoulders of her quilted coat.

"Get 'em out fast, Alvin!" Longarm swung back toward the window, gaining his heels and thumbing fresh shells from his belt and into the Winchester's loading gate. "I'll be along in a minute . . ."

Outside, Little-Boy was stealing up the porch steps, gritting his teeth with fury and swinging his rifle and long-barreled Colt back and forth between the broken-out window and the front door. His glance found Longarm, and he triggered both weapons at the same time. Longarm jerked back behind the window frame as the two slugs chewed slivers from the outside casing.

Longarm swung his Winchester around the window. Little-Boy was cocking his own rifle with one hand while thumbing back the revolver's hammer. His eyes met Long-arm's, then dropped to the maw of the rifle protruding two feet from the broken window. Realizing Longarm had the drop, he loosed an enraged bellow and began swinging both weapons toward the window.

Longarm squeezed the Winchester's trigger.

As the slug tore through the big Indian's round belly between the open flaps of his buffalo robe, Little-Boy triggered his rifle and revolver into the porch floor. He jerked forward, weapons tumbling out of his hands. His face crumpled, eyes slitting as he glanced down at the smoking hole in his gray flannel tunic.

Blood began welling from the hole. He looked up at

Longarm as though for corroboration that he had, indeed, just taken a .44-40 slug through his liver.

Longarm rose from his crouch, levered another shell into the Winchester's breech, and drilled two more slugs through the big man's chest, sending him flying straight back down the porch steps and into the street washed with the blood of the four other dead men.

Little-Boy ground his heels into the snow and arched his back, panting. He froze in that position, suspended on his shoulders and heels, then expelled one last chuff, dropped his back to the street, and died.

Several more soot-darkened men had dropped their water buckets and had come running toward the whorehouse. Only two held revolvers. Longarm racked a fresh shell, stepped over the window casing onto the porch, shouldered the rifle, and fired four quick rounds into the snow about two feet in front of the approaching men.

They'd formed a ragged wedge as they approached Miss Sylvania's, and that wedge stopped abruptly, boots sliding forward in the blown-up snow, the men spreading their arms for balance. They cast fearful looks toward Longarm, still aiming the Winchester over the porch rail, the butt pressed tight to his shoulder.

He expelled a spent shell. It clinked to the porch floor behind him. Racking a fresh cartridge, he continued squinting down the Winchester's barrel. "Miss Sylvania's is done closed till further notice."

Glaring up at him, the men slowly lowered their arms. All six wore prospectors' heavy ragged coats, cloth or fur hats, and hobnailed boots. To a man, their faces were bearded and scarred. One wore an eye patch like the one resting on Longarm's forehead.

Behind them, more concerned with saving the town

than with the commotion at the whorehouse, the other townsmen scurried around, throwing bucketfuls of creek water on the flames. They seemed to have the fire contained to the south side of town and only four buildings up from the livery barn.

The prospector nearest Longarm—as big as Little-Boy but with long, silver hair hanging from his bear hat—cursed loudly. He glanced at the others as he turned and began slouching back toward the fire and the bucket he'd dropped in the street.

"Let it go, goddamnit, fellas."

As the big man drifted off, others turned to reluctantly follow. A stocky blond gent with a shaggy handlebar mustache said above the flames' roar and the men's shouts, "You law?"

Longarm nodded once and flexed his fingers on the Winchester's forestock.

"Fuck," the blond gent said. He followed the others back toward the fire like a scolded schoolboy, head hanging.

Longarm lowered the Winchester and off-cocked the hammer. He stepped back through the broken window and tramped past Sylvania Thayer's carcass sagging back in the wheelchair as he headed toward the room's rear.

As his eyes adjusted to the dimness, he saw that six or seven half-dressed girls had gathered at the top of the stairs—females of all ages, shapes, and sizes and wearing shifts or dusters of all colors of the rainbow. Casey stood near the top left railing post, staring down grimly at the body of their fallen madam.

"Headin' for Alamosa. You girls are welcome to tag along if you like," Longarm said, shouldering his rifle and canting his head, squinting up the stairs. "Not much left for you here."

Casey and the other girls shared speculative glances. Casey turned back to Longarm, and shrugged a shoulder. "I reckon none of us has nowhere else to go. With Miss Sylvania and Little-Boy dead, we can finally start earning a grubstake here."

Longarm glanced around, then turned back to the girls. "As far as I'm concerned, the place is yours." With that he continued through the door to the right of the stairs, through a cluttered storeroom, and into the back alley. His mule stood tied to a hitch rail fronting a dilapidated stable on the alley's other side.

Mel, Alvin, Dominique, and the Chinese girls were gone, but the scuffed shoe tracks showed the direction they'd headed. Longarm mounted up and followed the trail westward. He'd ridden ten minutes when he saw a slender horseback rider sitting the trail before him, between walls of snow-flocked evergreens.

The girl's red hair fell to slender shoulders. Dominique's breath puffed into the air around her head. The horse's breath jetted from its nostrils as it stared toward Longarm, rippling its withers.

Sixty yards beyond the girl, Mel and Alvin led the Chinese girls up a long, low rise. Two of the girls, bundled and hunched against the cold, rode double. The third rode alone atop a leggy paint.

Longarm pulled up to Dominique's black. The pretty dove sat straight-backed, her mittened hands crossed on her saddle horn, and regarded Longarm grimly. "Is it finished?"

"It's finished."

Her lips parted and she loosed a long, heavy sigh. "Thank God." She slid a lock of hair from her eyes. "There's another village about eight miles down the mountains. They have a telegraph office and a narrow-gauge train that connects with the main line to Alamosa."

"What're we waitin' for?" Longarm heeled his mule ahead.

Dominique reached out and grabbed his arm. "Wait."

Longarm stopped.

Dominique blinked back tears. "I don't know how to thank you for getting me out of there," she said.

Longarm quirked a half grin. "I reckon you done thanked me plenty already. And I don't just mean by the way you cleaned Mojave Joe's clock, neither."

Dominique leaned far out from her saddle, wrapped an arm around his neck, and kissed him. She pulled away, and the light danced in her brown eyes. "There's plenty more where that came from, Deputy."

Longarm wrapped an arm around her, closed his mouth over hers. "Like I said—what're we waitin' for?"